"Better?" he asked so softly.

He was stroking her hair by then. It felt way too good.

She kept her head buried in his shoulder. "Yeah. Better. For the moment, at least." He smelled good. Clean. Like soap and cedar shavings. Like pine trees in the springtime. He'd always smelled like pine.

"What *was* that?" he asked. "Are you going to be okay?"

"Yeah. More or less," she panted, and she made herself look up at him, at his worried frown and his blue eyes full of questions.

She told him, "I'm in labor. The baby's coming. The baby's coming *now*...."

Dear Reader,

Some of you may recall that a few years back, in Brett Bravo's story, *Married in Haste,* Bowie Bravo left his hometown of New Bethlehem Flat, California, to try to make some kind of life for himself. He left behind a son named Johnny and his son's mother, Glory Dellazola. Glory loved Bowie deeply, but she just wouldn't marry him, no matter how many times he asked. Bowie was wild and undisciplined and not likely to change.

Now, almost seven years later, Bowie has turned his life around. And at last, he's come back to make things right. Too bad Glory has hardened her heart against him and his son has been calling another man Dad.

Bowie's got a lot to make up for. But he's a determined man now. He won't give up, no matter how hard Glory pushes him away.

Glory, recently widowed, has a new baby on the way. Bowie knows she needs him now. And his son needs him, too. He's not running away this time. Once and for all, he's going to prove that he's ready to be the man Glory always needed him to be.

Happy reading, everyone!

Yours always,

Christine Rimmer

THE RETURN OF
BOWIE BRAVO

CHRISTINE RIMMER

Harlequin®

SPECIAL EDITION

Recycling programs
for this product may
not exist in your area.

ISBN-13: 978-0-373-65650-9

THE RETURN OF BOWIE BRAVO

Copyright © 2012 by Christine Rimmer

Printed in U.S.A.

CHRISTINE RIMMER

came to her profession the long way around. Before settling down to write about the magic of romance, she'd been everything from an actress to a salesclerk to a waitress. Now that she's finally found work that suits her perfectly, she insists she never had a problem keeping a job—she was merely gaining "life experience" for her future as a novelist. Christine is grateful not only for the joy she finds in writing, but for what waits when the day's work is through: a man she loves, who loves her right back, and the privilege of watching their children grow and change day to day. She lives with her family in Oregon. Visit Christine at www.christinerimmer.com.

For Hazel Schwartz,
who kept after me for years
until I finally wrote Bowie's story.
Hazel, this one's for you!

Chapter One

Glory Rossi saw him coming. He seemed to materialize out of the storm.

It was a blustery Monday morning in mid-January and
she stood at the bay window in the family room at the
front of the house. She stared out at the snow that had
started coming down only a little while ago.

The wind whistled under the eaves outside, catching
the thick, white flakes and carrying them sideways in
drifts and eddies, so the world out there was a whirling
fog of white. She couldn't see much beyond the bare box
elder tree in the front yard—not the bridge across the
street that spanned the river, not the houses on the other
side. She knew her hometown of New Bethlehem Flat,
California, like she knew her own face in the mirror, but
the snow obscured it now. She thought how empty the
house seemed, how lonely and lost the wind sounded as
it sang under the eaves.

And then she caught a hint of movement within the white. She frowned. Squinting, she leaned closer to the glass.

No doubt about it. There was someone out there, a tall, broad-shouldered figure coming up the front walk. The figure mounted the steps.

Glory turned to look out the side window in the bay. It gave a view of the porch. A man, definitely. She couldn't see his face. His head was hunched into his down jacket and a watch cap covered his hair.

He stood at her front door and raised a gloved hand to ring the bell.

And right then, as the doorbell chimed, she *knew*.

It couldn't be. It wasn't possible. And yet, she was absolutely certain.

Bowie.

As if he felt her watching him, he turned her way. And he saw her, standing there at the window, her hand on the hard, round bulge of her belly, staring at him with her mouth hanging open.

No.

Her mind rebelled. Why now, after all this time? It made no sense. She must be dreaming.

He looked…different, the hard planes of his face more sculpted than before. He looked older. Which he was. By more than six years.

Older *and* sober. The gorgeous blue eyes were clear as the Sierra sky on a cloudless summer day.

Dreaming. Yeah. This had to be a dream.

She looked away from him, counted to five and then glanced back. Dream or not, he was still out there at the front door, watching her. Maybe if she did nothing, if she just stood there, frozen, refusing to move or even breathe no matter how many times he rang the bell…

Maybe he would give up and go away.

But she knew he wouldn't. In his eyes she saw a strange, calm determination. He wasn't going to simply turn and leave.

Seeing no other choice, Glory went to let him in.

In the foyer, she paused with her hand on the doorknob, certain that when she pulled open the door, there would be nothing on the other side but wind and snow. He would have vanished as suddenly as he'd appeared. She could return to her life as she had come to know it, could snap herself out of the funk that had gripped her that morning, and go about the mundane tasks that waited for her: doing the laundry and loading the dishes into the dishwasher.

Glory opened the door.

Snow blew in on a gust of wind, stinging her cheeks with icy wetness. She wrapped her arms around herself and shivered.

He was still there. He was absolutely, without-a-doubt real.

A soft cry tried to slip out of her throat. She swallowed it down and hitched her chin high. Beyond seeming taller and broader than she remembered, he also struck her as more…formidable, somehow.

"Hello, Glory," he said. He regarded her solemnly. His voice was the same, only deeper, richer.

A shiver went through her. It wasn't because of the cold.

Her heart rebelled. It wasn't right. Wasn't fair. After everything. All these years. After her sweet Matteo, who had shown her what peace and happiness could be…

It wasn't right. But apparently, rightness had nothing to do with it.

Six and a half years since he'd vanished from her life, Glory gazed up at Bowie Bravo and she knew that she still felt it for him. Even big as a barn with her lost husband's unborn child, she still had that *thing* for him.

She despised herself at that moment. And him, too.

"Are you going to let me in?" He asked it calmly. Gravely, almost. He seemed so different from the crazy wild man she used to know.

She considered simply closing the door in his face.

But what good would that do? In the end, since he had come, he would have to be dealt with.

She stepped back. He took off the watch cap as he crossed her threshold and she saw he'd cut his long blond hair. He wore it cropped close to his head now.

He removed his gloves and shrugged out of the down jacket. Underneath the jacket, he wore a faded chambray shirt with the sleeves rolled to reveal his corded forearms. His jeans were faded, too. "Where's Johnny?" he asked, sticking the gloves in a pocket of the jacket.

Her heart rate accelerated. Was she in for a custody battle? Was that what this sudden, out-of-the-blue visit meant? "He's in school."

"In this storm?"

Oh, please. Suddenly he was worried about Johnny? That was rich. "It's supposed to blow off by early afternoon."

"It's pretty wild out there."

"Yeah, well. The school will call if they decide to close. Besides, it's Trista's turn to pick up the kids." Trista was second-born of Glory's eight siblings. "She has four-wheel drive and some serious snow tires." Glory took his hat and jacket and hooked them on the coat tree at the foot of the stairs. Then, reluctantly, she offered, "You want some coffee?"

"Sure."

She led him through the door at the rear of the hall,

into the kitchen in back, where she gestured at the table in the breakfast nook. "Have a seat." He sat down and she made quick work of loading up the coffeemaker. "It'll be a few minutes."

"Fine."

"Are you hungry?"

"No, thanks. Just the coffee would be great."

She took the chair opposite him, lowering herself carefully into it, feeling huge and awkward in her maternity pants and a baggy shirt—and hating that she even gave a damn how she might look to him. "So have you been to see your mom?" Chastity Bravo owned the Sierra Star Bed and Breakfast down at the other end of the block, where Jewel Street met Commerce Lane.

"Not yet," he said. "I came here first."

Besides his mom, two of his three brothers—Brett and Brand—still lived in town. She'd never asked any of the Bravos—not even her own sister Angie, who was Brett's wife—where Bowie was or how she might reach him. In fact, after he'd been gone a year and a half, when she'd finally accepted that he wasn't coming back, she'd made it painfully clear to all of them that she was moving on with her life and she didn't ever again want to hear his name.

But that didn't mean that his family hadn't kept him up to date on her and Johnny. Somebody had told Bowie where she lived. She'd been getting checks from him for more than four years now, every month. Regular as clockwork.

Checks with a Santa Cruz postmark, checks that kept getting larger as time went by. Checks that scared her a little, if the truth were known. Where did he get all that money? It wasn't as though he'd ever managed to hold down a job.

And when she'd married Matteo and she and Johnny moved into this beautiful old house at the top of Jewel Street with him? Right away, that first month, Bowie's checks had started coming to their new address.

Bowie said, "How are you doing, Glory?" The question, which did sound sincere, fell into the long and painful silence between them. The silence of broken hearts. The silence of loss and love gone bad. The silence that happened when the best two people could do was to stay away from each other. And move on.

Bad enough, since I lost my husband. Worse, since you showed up.

She reminded herself that there was nothing to be gained by antagonizing him. "I'm all right." But she wasn't, not really. And already she was beyond tired of sitting here, trying to talk reasonably when the pain of the old wounds felt all too fresh and new again, when the truth of his desertion hung like a dirty gray curtain in the air between them.

The baby kicked. She winced and put her palm to her side.

He frowned and sat up a little straighter. "You okay?"

She blew out a breath. "Babies kick, but I guess you wouldn't have a clue about that."

He studied her from under those sun-gold eyebrows. "You're bitter. I can't say that's a big surprise."

"What do you expect, Bowie?"

"Of you? Nothing. Of myself? A lot more than I used to."

What was that supposed to mean? Her pulse pounded hard in her ears and her stomach felt queasy. She wanted to jump up and order him out of her house. Instead, she rose with slow care and went to the coffeepot. It was still dripping. But there was more than enough for a cup. She filled a mug, carried it back to the table and pushed it across to him.

"Thanks." He took it and sipped.

She lowered her bulging body into the chair again. "Look, can we just get real here?"

He rested one rough-knuckled hand on the tabletop. She watched as he traced a seam in the wood. And then he slanted her another of those strange calm looks. "I *am* being real." His voice stayed level, as composed as his expression. It scared her a little. Was this really Bowie sitting across from her? Bowie Bravo *never* stayed calm.

"What's up?" she demanded. "Just tell me. Why are you here?"

He took his sweet time answering that one, first picking up the cup again and taking another sip, then setting down the cup, then tracing that seam in the tabletop some more. "I figured it was about time I got to know my son."

Long past time, she thought, but she didn't say it. Over the years, she'd learned a little self-control, too. "Why now, exactly?"

"I've been—" he seemed to seek the right words "—trying to decide when the best time would be. Finally, I realized there was no good time." *No good time.* Well, at least she agreed with him there. "So I chose today." He added, "I heard you lost your husband. Matteo Rossi was a good man."

"Yes, he was," she shot back too fast and too angrily. New Bethlehem Flat, aka "the Flat" to everyone who lived there, had a population of around eight hundred. The Rossi family was an old and respected name in the Flat. Matteo had run Rossi's Hardware Emporium for half of his life. And before him, his father, Christopher, had owned the store.

Bowie said, "I'm…sorry that he's gone."

"So am I—and Johnny won't be home from school for hours yet." *And the last thing he'll be expecting is to see you here.* And really, how could this be happening? What exactly *was* happening? She still didn't get it. Her heart was working overtime, beating a sick rhythm under her ribs, the rhythm of dread. If he tried to take Johnny away...

But he wouldn't. He couldn't. No court in the world would give him custody of the son he'd made no effort to visit in almost seven years.

And no matter how much she might wish that he could have just stayed away, well, she knew what was right: he should know his son.

And Johnny needed to know him.

She asked, "How long are you going to be in town?"

"I'm keeping it open-ended." He leaned toward her a little.

She sat back, maintaining the distance between them. "Staying with your mom, at the B and B?"

"I'm not sure where I'll stay, Glory."

"Well, aren't you just a font of useful information?" It came out really sour-sounding. She turned to the window and watched the swirling snow beyond the glass, knowing she had to get a grip. Nothing would be gained by her playing the bitch about this. The past was a foreign country now. And so far, even though he wasn't telling her much about what his plans might be, he'd been perfectly civil. More so than she'd been, certainly.

"Glory, I'm sorry. I really am. Sorry about all of it, the thousand-and-one ways I messed things up." His voice was full of sadness.

She had no doubt he meant every word of what he'd just said. Still, she didn't look at him. "A letter, you know?" she said to the white world outside the window.

"A letter now and then. It would have meant so much to him. You couldn't even manage that?"

"Things were bad at first. I had to get sober and it wasn't easy. I told myself that when I was sober for two years, when I had some kind of handle on myself, on my behavior, I would get in contact, start trying to work things out. But then you married Matteo…"

She made a low, furious sound in her throat. "Oh, that's your excuse, then? That it's *my* fault you never got to know Johnny. My fault because I got married."

"I didn't say that."

"But it's what you meant."

"No, Glory. It's *not* what I meant. What I meant is I knew enough about Matteo Rossi to realize that he would be a good husband. I knew he was gentle and patient and kind. And he brought in a good income. He was pretty much everything that I'd never been. I thought that it would be the best thing, to stay away. To let you have a life, you know? Not to cause you any more trouble."

"A son needs to know his father." She hated to say it. It only supported his claim on Johnny, however late in time he'd returned to make that claim. Still, it was the truth.

"I see that now." His voice was soft. Reasonable.

She wanted to pop him a good one right in his too-well-remembered face. "He's a little kid," she accused. "He doesn't understand why his dad went away before he was even a year old, why you never came back. All a little kid knows when his dad disappears is that it must somehow be *his* fault."

His expression darkened. "I used to think that when I was a kid." His voice wasn't so gentle now and his square jaw was set. "I wanted my father to come back. I blamed myself that he didn't. But then I grew up and I learned more about him, enough to be glad I'd never met the rotten bastard."

"That was a completely different situation. You are not your dad."

"I'm just saying it's not absolute, Glory. Given who I was when I left town, Johnny *was* better off not knowing me."

"I don't believe that." She spoke low, with heat. "I'll never believe that."

"Just stop. Just think for a minute." His blue gaze pinned her.

"Stop and think about what?"

"You said you understood, don't you remember? You said that you were okay with it, when I left."

"I did understand. It's a small town. People make judgments. And here in the Flat, you were everybody's favorite screwup. You could never get anything right. They all expected you to mess up again, no matter how hard you tried not to. And you never disappointed them. I understood that you needed to get away, to get out from under that judgment, to figure out for yourself who you are, really. What I didn't expect was never to hear another word from you."

"You heard from me." He said it to the window.

"Checks in the mail are not 'hearing' from you."

Bowie sipped his coffee. He stared blankly out at the storm, the same way she had done a few moments before. Finally, he set the cup down—a little harder than necessary—and he turned his gaze on her again. "It's not like you ever came looking for me, not like you gave me any kind of sign that you wanted me around."

She met his eyes and she refused to look away. "It wasn't my job to make you feel *wanted.* It was *your* job to be a father to your son."

A muscle in his jaw twitched, but he kept his voice strictly controlled. "You don't give an inch, do you, Glory? You never did."

"I couldn't afford to. I had a son to raise."

"Ouch," he said, too softly. And then he continued, "The good news is, I *do* get what my job is. And I'm ready to do it, to be a father to my son. You're not chasing me off this time, no matter what you say or what you do."

Her temper flared. "Meaning *I* chased you out of town before? You know that's not true."

"How many times did you refuse me, Glory? A hundred? A thousand?"

She stared him down. "Tell me to my face right this minute that you think a marriage between us would have been a *good* thing. You go ahead, Bowie Bravo. You tell me that lie."

He had the grace to look away. And then he brought up his big, rough yet heartbreakingly graceful hands, and scrubbed them down his face. "I didn't come here to do this, to play the blame game. I honestly didn't."

"Then stop," she commanded in a hissing whisper. "Just...stop." She shoved back her chair and lumbered upright. Too bad that once she was on her feet, she didn't know what to do next. So she turned and went to the counter. She got the coffeepot, brought it back to the table, held it up.

"Great. Yeah," he said.

She refilled his cup. It was an awkward moment, standing there beside him, pouring with her arm extended at an odd angle. She had to turn a little to the side so that her bulging stomach wouldn't touch him. She didn't think she could have borne that right then, to have her stomach and her baby inside it—Matteo's baby—touching Bowie Bravo.

She managed to pour without spilling and also without any part of her body making contact with his. That accomplished, she took the pot back to the coffeemaker. Then she turned, leaned against the counter and told him, "You should know that Johnny and Matteo were close. Johnny loved his stepdad a lot."

Bowie gave one slow nod of his close-cut golden head. "That's good. For Johnny. And Johnny is the one who matters."

She took one step toward the table again—and that was when the contraction hit.

A full-blown, hard-labor contraction. Starting at the top of her uterus, it moved down and around, like huge and powerful hands, tightening, pressing....

Stunned at the suddenness of it as much as at the pain, she cried out, "Oh!" and staggered.

"My God. What the..." Bowie shot to his feet and started for her. "Glory..."

She clutched her belly with one hand and put out the other to ward him off. "I...no." She tried to deny the reality of what was happening. Anything to get him to stay back, not to touch her. "Really, I'm fine, I..." The sentence died unfinished. All she could do was groan deep in her throat as the contraction kept squeezing, as it got even stronger. It had her in a vise grip, until she couldn't hold herself upright any longer. She had to turn and bend over the counter to keep from sinking to her knees.

"Glory..." He came at her again and that time, she didn't have the presence of mind to back him off. All at once, he was there, touching her, putting his arms around her, supporting her as she rode out the pain.

There was a minute—or two or three—an endless, animal space of time when she didn't even care that Bowie Bravo had his hands on her again. All she knew was the pain, all she cared about was to ride it, to get through it and come out on the other side.

When it finally faded and left her panting for breath, the relief was the sweetest thing she'd ever experienced. By then, she was sweating and holding on to him. She couldn't help it. She needed someone to hold on to and he was the only one there.

"Better?" he asked so softly. He was stroking her hair by then. It felt way too good.

She kept her head buried in his shoulder. "Yeah. Better. For the moment at least." He smelled good. Clean. Like soap and cedar shavings. Like pine trees in the springtime. He'd always smelled like pine.

"What *was* that?" he asked. "Are you going to be okay?"

"Yeah, more or less," she panted and made herself look up at him, at his worried frown and his blue eyes full of questions. She told him, "I'm in labor. The baby's coming. The baby's coming *now*...."

Bowie's tanned face blanched. His eyes, too, seemed to lose their color, to grow paler. She looked in those eyes and she thought of his father, for some crazy reason. She'd never seen Blake Bravo in the flesh. He'd made his last visit to the Flat before she was born. But she'd seen the pictures, heard the stories. People said that Bad Blake Bravo, kidnapper, suspected murderer and notorious polygamist, had the kind of eyes you never forgot.

Pale eyes, wolf eyes...

Bowie was staring at her, blinking like a man suddenly wakened from a deep sleep. "Uh, what did you say? Tell me you didn't say what you just said."

She had the most ridiculous urge to laugh. "Sorry, I did say it. And it's true. My baby's coming." Strange how absolutely certain she was. But then again, she'd been here before. "It's just like it was with Johnny. Out of nowhere, with zero warning, I was far gone in labor. He was born an hour and a half after I had my first contraction—one that felt exactly like the one I had just now."

"You're not serious."

"Oh, yes, I am. This baby is coming. And coming fast."

Chapter Two

"Now?" Bowie cast a desperate glance toward the windows. Outside, the wind gusted and the snow came down harder than ever.

"Yeah, Bowie. Now." She could almost feel sorry for him. This had to be the last thing he'd expected when he came knocking on her door.

He gulped. "The hospital. I've got to get you to the hospital."

She shook her head. "In this storm, on the mountain roads? It would take forever to get there. And this baby is just like Johnny. This baby is not going to wait."

He remembered. She could see it in his eyes. He'd been there when Johnny was born—or at least, he'd tried to be there. She'd had Johnny in her mom's house down the street, upstairs, in the big front bedroom. Bowie had begged her to marry him as she sweated and screamed through one grueling contraction after another. He'd pleaded and he'd coaxed. He'd been drunk, as he usually was back then. His brother Brett, who was the town doctor, had finally gotten him to go away.

But he wasn't drunk now. He said, "The emergency helicopter. We can have you airlifted."

"Come on, Bowie, nobody's flying a helicopter in this." She flicked a hand toward the storm outside.

"Brett…" He said his brother's name desperately. She understood that, the desperation. She wanted cool, calm, competent Brett there, with her, and she wanted him now. And when Brett came, so would her sister Angie. Angie was not only Brett's wife, she was also his nurse. And of her six sisters, Glory had always felt closest to Angie. She could tell Angie anything. They were not only siblings, they were also best friends.

The phone was a few feet away down the counter. Going for it gave her an excuse to escape the scarily comforting circle of Bowie's arms. She had the number of Brett's clinic on auto dial, so she punched it up fast.

The receptionist answered on the second ring. "New Bethlehem Flat Clinic. This is Mina."

"It's Glory, Mina. I'm in labor. The baby's coming and coming fast."

"No kidding? Wow. Right now? Isn't that a little early?"

Glory gritted her teeth. "Yeah, Mina. It's two weeks early, but it's happening. I need Brett and Angie over here at my place, now."

"They're out on a call." A call. Sweet Lord. They were out on a call. Mina chattered on. "Scary, huh, in this weather? But evidently, Redonda Beals and Emmy Ralen just had to go out for their morning walk today of all days. The storm started. Redonda took a fall. Broke her arm in two places. It's pretty bad, evidently. Dr. Brett is seeing what he can do about it until the weather clears and she can be airlifted to Grass Valley."

"Can you reach them, tell them I'm going to need them over here, and fast?"

"They should be back soon—I mean, unless the snow keeps up like this."

"Mina, hello. I asked if you would call them."

Bowie moved closer, frowning. "Let me talk to her."

Glory put her palm over the mouthpiece and told him drily, "Thanks, I can handle this."

He stopped coming toward her, but he kept on frowning.

Mina was gabbing away again. "Now, Glory, I have kids of my own. I know how long labor takes. And I know sometimes you feel it's urgent when really it's going to be quite a while."

Oh, great. Just what she needed. Lectures on childbirth from Mina Scruggs. "Mina, forget it. Are they at Redonda's? I'll look up the number and call them myself."

"Glory, there is no reason to get snippy."

"I am having my baby, Mina. I am having my baby *now.*"

Mina made a humphing sound. "How far apart are your contractions?"

As Mina said the operative word, another one hit— worse than the first one. It started at the top of Glory's stomach and it moved downward, a deep, clutching, hard pain, gathering and pressing as it moved. She groaned and almost hit her forehead on the counter as she doubled over with the force of it.

"Glory! Glory, you still there?" Mina called from the other end of the line.

Bowie took the phone and growled into it. "She's having a contraction. A strong one. You need to get Brett here right away..." Mina said something. He made a low sound. "Who am *I*? Bowie... That's right, Mina. Bowie Bravo... Yeah. Right. I'm back in town. Surprise, surprise. Now don't you be messin' with me. Get my brother over here and get him here right now...."

Glory tuned out the rest. She was too busy riding that contraction all the way to hell and back and swearing a blue streak as she went.

She didn't normally have a filthy mouth, but there was something about giving birth. It brought out every bad word she'd ever heard and some she couldn't believe she knew.

When that one finally passed, Bowie had already hung up. He reported, "Mina will call them and tell them. They'll get in touch."

Her hair was already damp with sweat. Ugh. She swiped it back off her clammy forehead. "When, damn it?"

"She said she'd call them right away."

"Okay. Great." With care, pressing a hand to her back, she straightened up.

He looked down at the phone he held and then up at her. "Do you want to...go to your bedroom, get a little more comfortable?"

Oh, God. Having her baby. With only Bowie to help. "Bet you wish you'd picked another day to make your big appearance, huh?"

He stared at her for what seemed like a very long time. And then he said, "Well, I'm here. And I'll do what I can. Now, answer the question. You want to lie down or something?"

"Uh, no. Not right this minute." She bent at the waist and rested her head on the counter again. It was cool and smooth and felt good against her cheek. "I'll just stay here for now, wait for Brett to call, beat my head against the counter when the next contraction hits."

He looked stricken. "Don't even joke about it."

"Right." She blew out a hard breath through puffed cheeks. "Sorry."

He held up the phone. "How about your mom? Should I call her?"

Her mom. Good idea. Rose Dellazola knew a lot about having kids. She'd had nine of her own and been there at the births of every one of her grandchildren. "Yeah, please. It's number two on the auto dial—and Bowie?"

"Yeah?"

"Tell her if she brings Aunt Stella, I will personally kill both of them." Her maiden aunt, who lived with her mamma and her dad, was extremely devout. At births, Stella Baldovino spouted scripture and counted off the rosary—like she did pretty much everywhere she went.

He started to dial.

"Wait." Her cheek still pressed to the cool polished surface of the counter, she held out her hand. "I can do it."

He regarded her doubtfully. "Glory…"

She fisted her hand and pounded the pretty blue-speckled black granite that Matteo had ordered installed for her birthday last year. "Give me the phone. Now."

He handed it over. She braced up on her elbows and punched the right number. It rang three times and then the answering machine picked up.

"Hello," her mother's recorded voice chirped. "Dellazola residence. We do want to talk to you. Please leave a message and we'll get back to you as soon as we can."

Terrific. Her mom, her dad, her great-grandpa and Aunt Stella all lived in that house together. And they all had to choose today *not* to be home. Where had they gone in a blizzard?

She didn't even care to know. "Mom," she told the machine. "I'm having the baby. And I mean right now. When you get this, get over here to my house. I need you—and do not bring Aunt Stella. I mean that. Just don't." She turned the phone off and felt the next contraction coming on. "Bowie?" she moaned.

"Right here."

She cast a quick glance at the kitchen clock. It was ten after ten. "Watch the clock. The second hand. Starting now. Time this contraction..."

"Gotcha."

Glory started screaming. Bowie moved in close again. He held her up and he watched the clock. She heard herself swearing. Really bad words. Terrible words. It didn't make the pain any less, but she swore anyway.

When it faded, at last, she asked him, "Well?"

"Fifty-four seconds."

"Great," she said, for lack of any other reasonable response. She noted the time. "There's a pencil and paper in that little desk on the other side of the table. And a Timex watch with a second hand. Get them now." He didn't say a word. Just went over there and got what she'd asked for. She instructed, "Write down the time that contraction started and how long it lasted."

"Got it." He wrote on the paper.

"Do that every time I have one. Can you handle that?"

"Will do." He put on the watch and stuck the paper and pencil in a back pocket. "How about a cell phone? Your mom got one? We could try it. Or maybe Angie or Brett has one?"

She shook her head. "My mom never bothered to get one. Angie has one, but they still don't work here in the Flat. The canyon walls block the signal. You have to go up to the heliport to get any bars."

"Is there someone else we should call?"

She thought of her three sisters who still lived in town: Tris, Clarice and Dani. She loved them all dearly, but she didn't see how having them there was going to help her much. She wanted Angie. And Brett. And failing them, her mother.

He said, "*My* mom?"

Chastity. Yeah. Chastity had been good to Glory over the years. They were friends. And she was definitely the best choice given the options. "Call her."

He did. "Not answering," he said after a minute.

Glory said a word so bad that it would have dropped her aunt Stella in a dead faint. "Where *is* everybody? They're always underfoot until the moment you need them."

Bowie left a message. "Mom, it's Bowie. I'm at Glory's house. Her baby's coming—fast. And there's no one to help. If you get this, she needs you to come over here right away." He hung up.

Glory shut her eyes and whispered prayerfully, "Please, Brett. Angie. Call me, get over here...."

The phone rang as if on cue. She held out her hand. Bowie frowned again but he passed it to her. "Angie?" she cried. "Angie, oh God, I'm so glad you—"

"Don't be alarmed," said a pleasant recorded voice. "Your credit remains excellent. I'm Amy from Credit Card Services and I'm calling to tell you—" Muttering yet another unacceptable word, Glory hung up.

"What?" Bowie demanded, looking slightly freaked.

"Robo-call." She passed the phone back to him. "Call Mina again, please. See what the holdup is." She sighed and laid her head back on the counter as he called the clinic.

When he hung up, he said, "Mina tried to reach Brett

and Angie. Twice. It looks like the phone's out at Redonda's house. She got dead air when she called over there. She said she'd keep trying."

"I don't believe this."

"Maybe we should just try 9-1-1, see if we get some help that way," he said.

"Do it."

He started to dial, then put the phone to his ear. "We're out, too." He switched it off and then on again. "Nothing. Deader than a hammer." He handed it to her.

She listened. And heard only silence. The storm must have knocked down some lines. "No," she cried. "Oh, no...." Shoving the useless phone away down the counter, she lowered her cheek to the granite again. "This isn't real," she moaned. "This can't be happening...."

He loomed above her, wearing that determined look, the same one he'd worn when he stood at her front door. "You don't look comfortable bending over the counter like that."

She rolled her eyes and stayed right where she was. "I'm about as comfortable as I'm going to get, considering the circumstances."

"I think we probably ought to get you to the bedroom, I really do. And shouldn't I be boiling water or something?"

"Boiling water. He wants to boil water...." She let out a laugh that was almost a sob. "I'm having a baby and there's no one to help me."

"There's me. I think you're going to have to work with what you've got," he said with more humor than she could have mustered at that point. "For the moment, I'm it. You're going to tell me what to do and everything is going to be fine."

"Tell you what to do?" She pretty much screeched the

words. "How can I tell you, Bowie? I don't even know myself."

"You've had Johnny."

"Yeah, with Brett there to tell me when to push, with Angie there to hold my hand and coach me through every contraction...."

"You'll figure it out. *We'll* figure it out."

Glory yearned to call him a bunch of bad names and scream at him that he didn't know his ass from up. Unfortunately, he had a point. They would *have* to figure it out. There was no other choice. She had a couple of books on pregnancy and childbearing. One of them was bound to have a section on emergency births at home. They would refer to the chapter, follow the damn instructions.

She muttered out of the side of her mouth, "I hate you, Bowie Bravo."

"I know." He took her shoulders and pulled her off the counter and upright again. "Let's go."

Redemption, Bowie thought as he coaxed Glory up the stairs to her bedroom. That was pretty much what he'd come back to his hometown to get.

He wanted to know his son and to try, at least a little, to be an actual father, the kind he'd sure never had. To maybe make peace with Glory. And to help her however he could, with Johnny, with the new baby, with the damn hardware store she'd inherited from Matteo Rossi, if it came to that. He'd had this idea he'd do whatever was needed to make up for all the years he hadn't been there when his son and his son's mother needed him.

He hadn't gotten off to such a great start, he had to admit. She'd started out mad at him and then gotten madder.

And then, all of a sudden, she was screaming and

clutching her big stomach. She was having her baby. Now. Today.

Way to go, Bowie. He showed up, and instantly Glory went into labor. The doctor, the nurse and her whole family turned out to be unavailable. It was too dangerous to try driving to the hospital. Cell phones didn't work and the landline was dead.

It was all his fault, for showing up when he probably should have just stayed away. For pissing her off so bad that she started having contractions.

Redemption at this point didn't seem all that possible. In fact, it seemed like a ridiculous thing for him to have imagined he wanted, a silly crock of crap.

Right now, redemption didn't matter in the least. Glory was having her baby. And if anything happened to her or the child, well, he knew damn well whose fault *that* would be.

Halfway up the stairs, she had another contraction. She leaned over the railing, holding on to it with one hand and him with the other. She had quite a grip on her for a small woman. She gritted her teeth and yowled. And she swore. A long, harsh stream of amazingly bad words.

"Time?" she demanded when she stopped swearing. She blew a hank of sweaty brown hair out of her big brandy-colored eyes and looked at him like she dared him to answer that question.

But he was ready. He had the watch and he'd actually remembered to glance at the second hand when that one started. He told her—both the length of the contraction and the time between it and the one before it. And then he pulled the paper and pencil from his pocket and wrote everything down.

Once that was dealt with, he wrapped his arm around her again and coaxed her the rest of the way up the stairs.

The master bedroom was at the front of the house, big, with bay windows the same as in the family room below it. It had a separate sitting area, its own bath and a walk-in closet. All so damn tasteful, wallpapered in blue-and-white stripes, with sheer curtains and antique furniture that had probably been in the Rossi family—in that very house—for generations. He thought of Glory and Matteo sharing the big four-poster mahogany bed and then decided *not* to think about that.

She'd been happy with him, that was what mattered. He'd made her happy and he'd been good to Johnny. And he'd left her well set up when that sudden rock slide hit his car last summer and rolled him right off the road into the river gorge way below.

"There are going to be fluids," Glory said.

He didn't know whether to laugh—or run down the stairs and out the front door and never again let himself even consider coming back to the Flat and trying to make things right. "Good to know."

"We need a sheet of something plastic to protect the mattress."

"A shower curtain?"

"Good. The curtain liner in Johnny's bathroom is plastic." She pointed. "It's across the hall."

He ran in there and started ripping the inner curtain liner off the hooks, aware in a distant sort of way of the clothes hamper by the door with the leg of a pair of boy's jeans hanging out of it, of the bright plastic toys in the corner bin, of the jungle mural on the wall across from the old-fashioned claw-foot tub.

The task should have been simple, but the curtain hooks didn't seem to want to let go.

"Bowie?" Glory called from across the landing.

"I'm coming!" After forever, he had the damn thing free. He dragged it out of the bathroom and across the hall.

"About time," said Glory. She was kneeling in the sitting area, her head on a chair, a hand under the giant curve of her belly. "I was starting to wonder if you'd decided to have a shower while you were in there...."

"Sorry, I..."

She put up a hand. He knew from her expression that another one was starting. He dropped the curtain liner, checked the time on the watch and went to kneel beside her.

One hour later, the phone was still out and the snow was still coming down. No one had come to their rescue—not Brett and Angie, not Rose, not Chastity. Bowie had already volunteered to go down the block knocking on doors to see if anyone was around who might be able to help.

Glory had grabbed his hand. "If you leave right now, I will curse you until the day you die."

So he'd stayed. He'd found the place in one of her pregnancy books that told what to do in an emergency delivery.

He'd followed the instructions to the letter, stripping the bed and covering it with the plastic, and then covering the plastic with an old sheet. Between contractions, he'd coaxed Glory into the bathroom for a quick shower and then had her put on a T-shirt with nothing on under it.

She hadn't put up any argument about being pretty much naked in front of him. It wasn't like that, not in the least. It was just about doing the job of getting her baby born. Getting through it with both her and the baby safe and well.

He'd washed his hands thoroughly. And more than once, too.

He had two stacks of towels ready and another of clean, ironed receiving blankets from the baby's room. And ice chips. Between contractions, he'd bolted downstairs to the kitchen and gotten them for her, like the book said, so she could keep hydrated.

Every contraction had been timed and recorded—just in case a miracle happened and Brett showed up before the actual delivery and wanted the numbers on how far her labor had progressed. The contractions kept getting longer and closer together. And while they were happening, Bowie spoke soothingly to her, just like the book said. He comforted her and reassured her, per the instructions.

She continued to swear a blue streak and scream like it was the end of the world. She also clutched his hand so hard that she almost cut off the circulation to his fingers.

Now and then, when she wasn't screaming, when things settled down for a minute or two and Glory closed her eyes and seemed to be dozing, he thought of how he should have been there like this for her and for Johnny, when Johnny came. He thought about how much he'd missed, how many ways he'd gotten it all wrong.

And then he thought about Wily Dunn. He'd lost Wily only two months ago. The old man had died nice and peaceful in his sleep on the day after Thanksgiving. But if Wily was still around, Bowie knew what he would say about now. *That is water under a very big bridge. Let it flow on by, son. 'Cause there sure ain't no bucket big enough to catch it.*

"Bowie?" Glory squeezed his hand. "Another one. Starting now…"

He checked the watch on his wrist and then she was

screaming and he stopped thinking about all that he'd done wrong—stopped thinking altogether. He said soft, soothing things and told her to take quick, shallow breaths and to go with it. Just go with it and keep on breathing.

An hour and fifteen minutes after he'd gotten her upstairs, she was all the way down at the end of the bed, her head and shoulders supported by a pile of pillows, her feet on two chairs, knees wide. Bowie knelt on the floor between them. It was the last place he'd ever expected to be on the day he returned to New Bethlehem Flat.

The top of the baby's head appeared. Bowie said what the book had told him to say. "Pant, don't push. Easy, easy…" Glory moaned and panted. She seemed pretty focused now, and she wasn't even screaming. She did mutter a string of bad words, though, as she blew out quick, short breaths and moaned and swung her head to get the sweaty hair out of her eyes.

He used his hands—washed again a few minutes before—to apply gentle pressure as the head emerged. The goal, the book said, was to keep the head from popping out suddenly. The faster, the better, Bowie thought. But, hey. He followed the instructions and told himself to be grateful that so far, everything was going pretty much the way the book said, which he took to mean that everything was going okay.

The head slid free. It was all scrunched up and covered in sticky white stuff. The tiny, distorted mouth opened. But no sound came.

He reassured Glory. "Good, good," he said. "Really good."

"What does that mean?" she demanded furiously. "*Good, good.* Hello? That could mean anything."

He glanced up into her sweat-shiny face. "It means that so far, we're doing fine." And then he was back to business again. Gently, he stroked the sides of the tiny nose and downward toward the neck. And then he went the other way, upward from under the chin, to expel mucus and amniotic fluid from the nose and the mouth. It worked. Slimy, gooey stuff came out.

"What's happening?" Glory moaned, straining to see. "Is the baby…"

"Fine. It's fine. Shh, now. Shh…"

"Don't you shush me, Bowie Bravo."

"Shh…" Next, as gently as he could, he took the baby's sticky head in his two hands. "Okay, Glory. Now. Push!" She stopped griping at him and started grunting and bearing down and he pressed the baby's head very carefully downward at the same time.

And it happened. Just like in the book. One shoulder slid out.

After that, it was all so quick that he didn't have time to do what the book said. Nature did it for him. The other shoulder slid out. And then the rest of the tiny body came sliding fast in a rush of fluid, so fast he barely had time to catch it, let alone have the receiving blanket ready.

Glory cried, "My baby, my baby…"

And he said, "It's a girl," and then the tiny little thing opened her mouth and let out a big yelp followed by a long, angry cry. He smiled. Just like her mother, the dark haired little scrap of a thing didn't hesitate to make her feelings known.

"Is she…"

"She's perfect, Glory. Just perfect, I swear it." He got a blanket and put the baby on it, still with the cord connected. The book had said not to cut it, to wait for the professionals.

Bowie was just fine with that. There was also something called the placenta that might or might not be popping out before help came. He sincerely hoped that he might get lucky and not have to deal with that.

Glory was crying. "Serafina Teodora," she sobbed. "After Matteo's mom. Sera. She's Sera...." Glory held out her arms. And Bowie put another blanket around the tiny, red, sticky little body, to make sure she stayed warm. And then he lifted her up to give her to Glory.

But right then, as he levered up on his knees, carefully raising her to put her in Glory's arms, trying to hand her over without pulling on the cord that still connected her to Glory, he looked down and saw that the baby was staring up at him.

The little thing was quiet now. Calm. Her eyes watched him so seriously from that tiny, red, old-person face. Her mouth was a round *O*.

It was like...she knew him. That little baby knew him.

And she accepted him, absolutely. Instantly. Unconditionally, unlike her mother and most everyone else in his hometown where he'd never managed to do anything right.

He, Bowie Bravo, was okay with Sera Rossi, no questions asked.

And inside him there was a rising feeling, all warm and good. Right then, for that too-brief moment, looking into that baby's eyes, he could almost believe that everything would come out right.

Chapter Three

Glory was crying, the tears sliding along her temples into her already-sweat-soaked hair. "Come on," she said softly now, still holding out her arms. "Come on, give her to me."

Bowie handed Sera over.

He got up and washed his hands. Returning to the bedroom, he went to the bay window. It was quiet out there, the sky a gray blanket, the street covered in white. The wind had died down and he could see across the river now. Smoke spiraled from the chimneys of the houses over there and people were already outside, shoveling walks, scraping off windshields. "The snow's stopped," he said.

"Ah," Glory replied, kind of absentmindedly. He looked over and saw she had the baby at her breast and she was stroking the little one's matted dark hair, smiling a tender, secret, mother's smile.

Bowie checked the phone to see if they had a dial tone yet. Nothing. Dead air.

So he went to work mopping up the floor with the towels he had ready. He cleaned up as best he could without making a lot of noise and disturbing the exhausted mom and the tiny girl in her arms.

Glory asked for some apple juice. "In the fridge, downstairs," she added softly.

He went down to get it. The doorbell rang as he was starting up the stairs again and the sound grated in his ears, made the muscles at the back of his neck jump tight. He didn't want to answer it. He wished they'd all just stayed away.

Everything was so peaceful now. He hated to ruin it.

And he knew it would be ruined the moment everyone started showing up and they all found out that Bowie Bravo was back in town.

"Bowie?" Glory called from above.

"It's all right. I'm getting it." And then he turned and went and pulled open the door.

His brother Brett and his sister-in-law Angie, each wearing heavy coats and snow boots, mufflers, wool hats and gloves, and each with a black medical-looking bag, stood on the other side.

Angie blinked her big brown eyes. "Bowie. Wow. Mina said you were here...."

"Hey, Ange." He faced his brother. "Brett." And he knew, just from the wary look in Brett's hazel eyes, exactly what his brother was thinking, *Not again.* As a matter of fact, he'd seen the same look in Angie's eyes. He didn't blame them. How could he? After all, they were both there the day that Johnny was born, when he'd been drunk as a skunk and nothing but trouble. "Look," he said levelly, "I'm stone sober and I'm only here to help."

Brett and his wife exchanged a look. And then Brett said, "Good enough."

Bowie stepped back and let them in. They set down their black bags and started taking off the layers of outerwear.

Brett said, "Sorry it took us so long. The phone was out at Redonda's all morning. We didn't have a clue Glory was in labor until we got back to the clinic twenty minutes ago."

"Who is it?" Glory shouted from upstairs.

Angie answered, "It's me and Brett. We're on our way up." She grabbed her bag and raced up the stairs.

Brett hung back. He asked Bowie quietly, "How's she doing?"

"She did great," Bowie answered. "She's a damn champion."

Brett looked puzzled. *"Did?"*

And then Angie called down from the second floor. "Brett, you won't believe this. You'd better get up here...."

Ten minutes later, Brett had cut the umbilical cord and checked over both mother and child. He'd said what Bowie pretty much already knew. That Glory and Sera were doing fine.

Brett looked at him with real respect, which Bowie couldn't help but find gratifying. It was a much better reaction than he'd expected.

"Little brother," Brett said, "you did an excellent job here."

Even Glory gave him a tired smile. "Yeah, you did. Thanks."

He looked in her big brown eyes and dared to think that maybe coming back hadn't been such a dumbass idea after all.

The placenta arrived. Bowie was very grateful that it had waited to make its appearance until Brett and Angie were there to deal with it. Angie packed it up in a cooler to take to some woman who made vitamins out of it for the new mother—or something like that. Bowie didn't really care to get the particulars on the subject.

He checked the phone again a few minutes later and got a dial tone. "Phone's back on," he said, in case anyone needed to know.

It rang the second he hung it up. He stepped aside and let Angie get it. It was Rose Dellazola, Glory and Angie's mom, known around town as Mamma Rose. Angie told Rose that Rose's new grandbaby had arrived safely and everything was fine. When she hung up, she reported that Rose and the others had headed for Grass Valley at the crack of dawn that morning. It had been rough going, getting back in the storm. But they'd made it safely and Rose was coming over right now to meet her new grandchild.

Bowie and Brett's mom called next. Angie repeated the happy news and then passed the phone to Bowie. "Your mom wants to talk to you."

He took it. "Hey, Ma."

"Bowie, it's so good to hear your voice." He could tell that she was smiling, just by her tone. And maybe getting a little misty-eyed, too. He'd kept in touch with her in the time he'd been away, even started calling her now and then in recent years. Twice in the past two years she'd visited him up in the Santa Cruz Mountains. She said, "You come on down the street and see me."

He wasn't going anywhere until Johnny got home. "I will, Mom. In a few hours."

"Shall I fix up a room for you?"

"I don't know yet."

"Think about it."

"I will."

He'd barely hung up when Glory's mom and dad—and her aunt Stella, too—arrived. He and Brett went downstairs to let them in. Brett answered the door and they all three looked like they were seeing a ghost when they caught sight of Bowie.

"Bowie!" Glory's dad, whom everyone called Little Tony, clapped him on the back. "Good to see you, man!" He actually seemed to mean it.

Mamma Rose and Stella were friendly enough, too. They'd always been civil to him. Back when Johnny was born and Bowie had hounded Glory for months on end to marry him, the older generation of Dellazolas were all on his side. They were good Catholics. They believed that a man ought to be allowed to do the right thing and marry the mother of his child.

Bowie did see the irony. He'd been so worried about everyone's reaction to his showing up. But Stella was more upset about Glory's phone message than she was about seeing Bowie Bravo back in town again. She clutched her rosary to her chest. "I am hurt. Terribly hurt. Glory said she didn't want me here. Why wouldn't she want me here?" And then she started quoting scripture. *"'And I will cleanse them from all their iniquity, whereby they have sinned against me; and I will pardon all their iniquities, whereby they have sinned, and whereby they have transgressed against me.'"* She turned her dark eyes on Bowie then. Probably because he was the biggest sinner in the front hall at that moment. "Jeremiah, thirty-three," she declared in a noble tone, "verse eight."

Mamma Rose, who was taller, thinner and prettier than her sister, patted Stella's shoulder. "Now, Stell, you can't go taking it personally. You know how Glory is."

Stella pursed up her lips and fingered her rosary. "Yes, I do, sadly enough."

Rose put an arm around her and gave her a quick squeeze. "You know what they say? *This, too, shall pass away.*"

Stella's reply to that was an injured, "Hmmph."

A minute later, the two women went upstairs and Glory's dad joined Brett and Bowie in the kitchen. Brett and Little Tony seemed right at home in Glory's house. Brett got a fresh pot of coffee brewing and Little Tony went through the cupboards and the fridge looking for snacks, coming up with some packaged cookies and a box of mini chocolate doughnuts.

They sat for half an hour or so, drinking coffee, eating the doughnuts and talking about the weather and the New Bethlehem Flat High School basketball team. Nobody seemed to want to get around to the big, fat elephant in the room—which was what was Bowie doing there and where the hell had he been for all this time?

And then Mamma Rose appeared. She loaded some food and juice on a tray and took it back upstairs.

Once she was gone, Little Tony finally broached the delicate subject. "So, tell me, Bowie, how you been for all these years?"

Bowie said he was doing okay, that he lived in Santa Cruz, up in the mountains.

"You find work?"

"I did. I'm a carpenter now."

"As in construction?"

"I build mostly furniture."

"Any money in that?"

"I make a living."

"Good. Good. And it's great to see you back in town."

"Yeah," Brett agreed. "Good to have you back."

Bowie figured that was probably the warmest welcome he was going to get—except maybe when he went down the street to say hi to his mother. He told himself to be grateful that a few people seemed glad to see him. For the rest of them, he would either earn their respect—or get along without it, as he'd been doing for all of his life.

Later, after Brett and Little Tony left, Bowie sat in Glory's kitchen for a while, wondering what he ought to do with himself now. The women were all upstairs with Glory and the baby, doing whatever women do after a baby comes. The kitchen clock and the Timex watch he'd used to time Glory's contractions both agreed that it was quarter of one. What time did school get out? Two? Three? Four?

He took off the watch and put it back in the drawer where he'd gotten it and then he wandered around downstairs for a while. It was a great house. He'd always admired it. The place was well over a hundred years old and still standing strong. There were built-ins—that little desk area in the kitchen, the dining-room china cabinet and the waist-high bookcases on either side of the family-room fireplace. The bookcases, like the mantelpiece, were hand-carved with flowers and vines.

Eventually, when he ran out of quality woodwork to appreciate, he put on his jacket and went outside. The storm had dropped about six inches of new snow, white and pure, stretching out over the wide field at the back of the Rossi house, all the way to where the pines started. Since the house was at the end of Jewel Street, where the street hooked to the northeast and then came to an end, there was a good deal of open land around it on the north and east sides. His breath pluming in the icy air, he stood at the base of the back-porch steps and looked up at the mountains that rimmed the town, all of them blanketed in snow-dusted evergreens.

His hometown. In some ways it still didn't seem real to him, that he was here, that he'd actually done it. Returned to the place of his childhood. The place where he'd grown up and made such a mess of everything.

After a moment, he shook his head. He started moving, trudging through the fresh, powdery snow, out to the big gray barn fifty feet or so behind the house.

The barn had windows. He wiped the snow off the panes and peered in. The structure had been divided. The smaller side was a garage for a riding mower and other yard equipment. The larger section was a workshop. Through one of the workshop windows, he saw a cot and a free-standing woodstove, as well as pegboards hung with tools and long, rough waist-high wooden workbenches. A fluorescent light fixture hung from a ceiling beam.

It wasn't bad. Big enough for both a place to work and a living area. His needs were simple. A cot to sleep in and a stove to keep him warm during the long winter nights. If he stayed, the workshop would suit him fine, although he'd have to have a phone installed because his cell wasn't going to be any use to him here.

But getting a landline put in was no biggie. The biggie would be getting Glory to go for it. He hardly felt confident on that point.

You've got zero hope of getting a yes if you never ask the damn question, Wily Dunn would have said.

Right, Wily. But it's Glory we're talking about here. Glory wouldn't give him a yes if her life depended on it.

Still. If he felt he had to, he would ask the question, anyway. He'd know better what his next step should be after a certain six-year-old got home from school.

He returned to the back porch, knocked the snow off his boots and went inside again. Angie and Stella were in the kitchen and something that smelled good simmered on the cooktop.

"Soup and a sandwich?" Angie asked. She looked at him warmly, he thought. And suddenly, he was grateful after all that he'd come today, that for once, he'd been there for Glory when she needed him—and that her sister knew it.

He realized he was starving. "Soup and a sandwich would be great."

Angie fixed his food and he sat down to eat while she and her aunt loaded up a couple of trays and went back upstairs.

After he ate, he started wondering how Glory and little Sera were doing. He went out into the front hall and stood at the base of the stairs with a hand on the newel post and thought about going up there. He wanted to go up, but he didn't quite dare to. Instead, he went into the family room and rebuilt the fire that had burned down to coals during Sera's birth.

He'd just gotten it going good when he heard the front door open. He shut the door to the fireplace insert, hung the poker back on the stand and rose to his feet. The front door closed. Hesitant footsteps came closer. And stopped. He turned slowly to face the sturdy, handsome boy who stood in the arch to the foyer.

Still in his coat and hat, his rubber boots and backpack, the boy had Glory's brown hair and big eyes. And the telltale Bravo cleft in his square chin. He took his time, looking Bowie up and down.

Bowie returned his stare. The only sound was the crackle of the newly revived fire at his back. For Bowie, in that wordless moment, the world seemed to shift on its axis. Everything came into sharper perspective. He saw what he'd already known in his mind. But now he saw it through his heart and whatever that thing was that might be called a soul. Only at that moment did he fully accept that he had a job to do here, a job he'd left undone for too long.

There was no way he could leave town. Not in the near future anyway.

"I know you," the boy said at last, his mouth that was the same shape as the mouth Bowie saw when he looked in the mirror, curved in a sneer. "I've seen your pictures in Granny Chastity's house. You're the one they call my dad. But you're *not* my dad. My dad died. And I hate you."

Chapter Four

Bowie stared at the son who'd just said he hated him and tried to think of an acceptable reply.

There was none. Anything he said right then would only be so much crap.

Johnny didn't wait for him to think up something meaningful. He demanded, "Where's my mom?"

"She's...resting."

Johnny dropped the backpack down one arm. It plunked to the hardwood floor, although he still held it by a strap. "In her room?"

"That's right."

Hefting the pack, Johnny turned for the stairs.

"Wait."

The boy whirled back. "Don't you tell me what to do."

Bowie almost smiled. It was the kind of thing he used to say a lot—and not only when he was six. He thought of his own mom, for some reason. Of Chastity's calm, matter-of-fact approach to things. She used to be the only one with a chance of getting through to him. She never fought fire with fire. He said quietly, "Your sister was born this morning."

The boy tried to keep sneering, but his eyes went wide. "Is my mom okay?"

"Your mom is fine. Resting, like I said. Your aunt Angie, your grandma Rose and your great-aunt Stella are with her."

"What's her name, the baby?"

"Serafina Teodora, but your mom calls her Sera."

"I want to go up there. I want to see my mom and the baby."

"Take off your coat and hat and boots first. And go quietly. Remember to knock."

The boy did what he was told. He unzipped his jacket and took off his hat. Bowie marveled. At six, Johnny had more self-control than Bowie had possessed at twenty-six. The boy turned and left the archway.

Bowie didn't follow. Getting too close so soon seemed like a bad idea.

From where he stood at the fireplace, Bowie had a clear view into the front hall. He watched Johnny set his pack at the base of the coat tree, hang his jacket on a low hook and put his boots side-by-side next to his pack.

In stocking feet, Johnny went up, not looking back. Once he disappeared from view, Bowie moved to the foot of the stairs. He heard Johnny knock on his mother's door, a gentle, careful sort of knock.

And then he heard the door open and Mamma Rose's voice. "Here's our big boy...."

Johnny said something. Bowie couldn't make out the words. He heard the door click shut.

There was an easy chair by the fire. Bowie returned to the family room and sank into that chair. He sat and stared at the flames and waited for his son to come back downstairs.

It didn't take all that long. Fifteen minutes, maybe, and he heard the light step descending.

Bowie stayed in the chair. He had the feeling that sudden moves on his part would not be appreciated. Better to continue to keep his distance for a while. He might even get lucky and the kid would come to him.

Doubtful, but you never knew. So he waited.

The light footfalls came closer. "My mom says I have to be nice to you." The boy had stopped maybe six feet from Bowie's chair. He'd put on a pair of tennis shoes while he was upstairs.

Aware of a strange tightness under his breastbone, Bowie drank in the sight of him. "Did you see your sister?"

Johnny nodded. "She's pretty ugly. All red and wrinkled."

"Most babies are like that. But personally, I think she's gorgeous."

"You maybe need glasses, huh?" Johnny tipped his dark head to the side, frowning. "Are you a drunk and a crazy man?"

Bowie wanted to laugh. He also felt the burn of a more painful emotion sting the back of his throat. "Not anymore," he said. "But I used to be."

The boy seemed to consider that answer. And then he shrugged. "Mom says I can have milk and two graham crackers and then do my homework."

"Need any help with that?"

Johnny blew out a disgusted breath. "I'm not a *baby*."

"Well, I'm here if you need anything."

The look the kid gave him then was more puzzled than anything else. The big brown eyes said, *Why would I need anything from you?* And then he turned for the door to the kitchen.

Bowie should have left it alone then. He knew that. But somehow, he just had to say, "I'm going down the street to say hi to your grandma Chastity. Do you want to come with me?"

"No," the boy said. He neither paused nor looked back.

What did you expect? He hates you, remember?

Once Johnny disappeared into the kitchen, Bowie got up and climbed the stairs. He knocked on the door to Glory's room.

After a minute, Rose opened the door wide enough to put her head through the crack. She whispered, "Everything okay?"

"Just wanted you to know I'm going down to Ma's. Back in an hour or so. Johnny's in the kitchen."

"You look good," his mom said when she opened the door to him. "Healthy. Strong."

She looked pretty much as he remembered her, tall and slim in khaki trousers, a button-down shirt and a thick wool cardigan. Her short brown hair had more gray than before, and the lines bracketing her mouth and fanning out from the corners of her dark eyes were etched deeper than they had been. She was a practical woman who took care of business and of those she loved.

She stepped aside and he went in, accepting the hug she offered, then pulling back, holding her by the shoulders as she beamed up at him.

He said, "Good to see you, Ma."

"Take off your coat. Come on back."

He shrugged out of his jacket and she hung it in the closet by the door.

The Sierra Star Bed and Breakfast was as he remembered it. Homey and welcoming. A couple of people he didn't recognize sat on the sofa in the living room reading the town's weekly paper, *The Sierra Times.* Guests. They glanced up and smiled as his mom led him to the kitchen, her private domain at the back of the house.

She offered lunch, but he told her he'd eaten. He shook his head when she raised the full coffeepot in his direction.

So she poured herself a cup and sat in the chair opposite him. "Serafina Teodora, huh? It's a big name for a little baby."

"After Matteo's mother," he said.

Chastity made a low sound. "The saintly Serafina, who made sure her son had no other women in his life until she was in the ground."

"Come on, Ma, cut it out. I always liked Matteo. He was a fair man. Kind. And Glory and Johnny both thought the world of him."

"Did I say a thing against him? Not I. I liked Matteo. He and I were friends."

"I don't remember that."

"You were too busy getting into trouble to pay any attention to how often Matteo showed up around here."

"Here? You mean at the Sierra Star?"

Chastity nodded. "Believe it or not, Matteo even confided in me back in the day. We shared some really good…talks."

Bowie wondered what she was getting at. "What kind of 'talks'?"

"Private ones."

"Sheesh, Ma. Be a little mysterious, why don't you?"

"It hardly matters now. What matters is that Glory was happy with him. And he was good to Johnny. Wanted to

adopt him. Glory kept putting him off on the adoption
question, though."

"I didn't know that."

"See? There are real benefits to keeping in touch."

He let the dig pass because he was still stuck back
there with the idea that Matteo had wanted to adopt
Johnny. Bowie wasn't sure how he felt about that. Not
surprised, really. And not particularly happy, either. "For
Matteo to adopt my son, Glory would have had to come
to me, to deal with me."

His mom looked at him sideways. "I give her more
credit. I say she knew it would be wrong to cut you out
of Johnny's life that way."

"Maybe you forgot. She didn't even give him my
name." On Johnny's birth certificate, Glory had told Brett
to put Dellazola as the last name.

"But she did put you down as the father, didn't she?"

"Why are we talking about this, Ma?"

"You'd rather we discussed the weather? All right. It
was snowing. Now it's not."

He laughed. "Smart-ass."

"Don't call your mother names." Her old cat, Mr.
Lucky, jumped into her lap. She scratched him under the
chin. "People will think that you're badly brought up."

"I hate to break it to you, but I have a feeling they think
that already."

Her expression grew serious again. "You've got quite
a job ahead of you."

"I know it."

"Not only with Johnny." She stroked Mr. Lucky's
caramel-colored coat. "Glory's got that big heart of hers
hardened against you."

"That's not news—and it doesn't matter, about Glory's
heart. It's over between her and me. I just want to help

her out if I can because I owe it to her. And because she's the mother of my son."

"Oh, come on, you don't really believe that, do you? I certainly don't."

He reminded himself that his mother never did have her head screwed on straight when it came to love and romance. After all, she'd loved Blake Bravo. Loved him big time, and loved him long enough to give him four sons.

Chastity spoke again. "I know what you're thinking. Stop."

He said, "Glory loved her husband. I'm old news."

His mom looked into her coffee cup, but then set it down without taking a sip. Mr. Lucky jumped from her lap and strutted off down the hall. "How long you here for?"

"As long as it takes to work things out with my son and to see that Glory's back on her feet and managing okay with a new baby to look after."

"I wouldn't say she's on her own. She can't walk down the street without tripping over a relative."

"You know what I mean."

"Oh, yes, I do," his mom said too sweetly. "Probably better than you."

Back at Glory's house, he found Mamma Rose at the cooktop in the kitchen with a very fussy Sera on her shoulder. "Stella and Glory had words," she said with a shrug. "So Stell went home. Then Angie left, too. She's got the boys and Brett to look after." Angie and Brett had two sons—Jackson, who would be six in a couple of months, and Graham, who was two. Rose stirred a big pot of pasta sauce. "Johnny's upstairs in his room...." Sera let out a yelp, then yawned, then yelped some more.

"Stir this," she instructed. "I'll take this baby back up to her mamma."

"I'll take her up," he volunteered.

Rose sent him a doubtful look. "You sure?" He already had his arms out. "Well, you did deliver her. I guess you can manage to carry her upstairs well enough." Rose handed over the tiny pink-blanketed bundle.

Sera was light as a breath of air. And still squalling— until he had his arms around her. Then she did that thing again, same as the moment she was born. She blinked and looked up at him and her mouth was a round little *O*.

He grinned down at her. "Hey, how you doin' there, Sera?"

Rose took the diaper off her shoulder and put it on his. "She likes you."

Carefully, he lifted the tiny form and put her against his chest. She made a soft, cooing sound. And then she burped. He patted her on the back.

"Gently, now," said Rose.

"Yes, ma'am." He sent Glory's mom a grin.

Rose asked the question that seemed to be on everyone's mind. "How long you staying in town?"

"Not sure yet."

Rose looked like she maybe wanted to say more, but she only told him, "Watch the baby's head, now. She can't hold it up by herself yet."

He turned for the door to the stairs.

On the second floor, he saw that Glory's door was closed. So was another one across the hall—Johnny's room, he was reasonably certain. Because Sera was quiet in his arms, he was tempted to try Johnny's door first, take the baby in there, maybe let her brother hold her for a minute.

And maybe make the first small step toward getting to know his son.

But first things first. He needed to talk to Glory, to try and settle a few things while he had the chance. Over the next few days, it was going to be a challenge getting her alone. The Dellazola women would be looking after her and Sera round-the-clock—which only proved what his mother had said. She had family to take care of her and he wasn't really needed.

Didn't matter. He would find ways to make himself useful. What mattered, he kept telling himself, was that he was here, finally. And he wasn't going away until he'd righted all the things he'd made wrong.

He steadied Sera on his arm and gave Glory's bedroom door a tap.

"It's open," she called.

He went in as she reached out and switched on the lamp. She lay in the bed, which was all made up now with clean sheets and blankets.

"Bowie," she said grimly at the sight of him. Her expression asked the question she didn't actually put into words. *You still here?* She sat up against the pillows. Her hair looked a little better, not quite so tangled and stringy, like maybe she'd run a comb through it a couple of times. She wore a soft blue pajama top. He didn't know what she wore on the bottom because the blankets covered the lower half of her body. A white bassinet waited by the bed.

He carried Sera over to her. "She was fussing...."

"Here." Glory held out her arms. With care, he passed the baby to her. She started unbuttoning her pajama top.

Bowie took that as his cue to go to the bay window and looked out at the dark street in front. In the light of a streetlamp, he stared at a tangle of snow-covered blackberry vines on the far side, at the edge where the shoulder dropped off into the river gorge below. When he was a kid, during the long summer days, he used to pick the blackberries that grew on those vines. They were always small and covered with dust.

After a minute or two, he figured she'd had enough time to fiddle with her top and put the baby to her breast, so he turned to her again and found her watching him. He stuck his hands in his pockets. "So how are you feeling?"

"Like somebody ran me over with an eighteen-wheeler." She smoothed Sera's blanket, touched her round cheek with a brush of a finger. Then she glanced up at Bowie again. Her soft look turned instantly wary and her wide, full mouth drew tight. "Got something on your mind?"

He went for it. "That barn out back?"

"What about it?"

"I looked in. On the workshop side, there's a cot and a woodstove. I'd like to stay there, while I'm in town."

She raked her fingers back through her hair. "If you're staying for a while, can't you just go to your mom's?"

"I need a place to work."

"What do you mean work?"

"I'm a carpenter. I need a workshop."

"You want to build furniture out in the barn?"

"That's right."

"I'm sorry. This is a lot to take in. And I have to ask…"

"What?"

"Well, just like that, you can leave your job and move in here?"

"I have my own company, okay? I've arranged it so I can be away for a while."

"Your own furniture company? In Santa Cruz?"

"Yeah, more or less."

She made a scoffing sound. "Which is it? More? Or less?"

"Look, it's a long story and we probably don't need to go into it now."

"Oh, well, I hear that."

He gave her a long, slow look. And when he spoke, he kept his voice even. "Six months after I left town, I hit rock bottom."

"But you *weren't* drinking when you left town," she reminded him angrily. "You'd been sober for over a month."

"Well, I started again after I left. That's how it goes with alcoholics. It takes only one drink and I had that drink. And the next one. And the one after that. The day before my life finally started to change, I ended up drunk on my ass at this weird party up in the Santa Cruz Mountains and—"

"What does some party in Santa Cruz have to do with your owning a business?" she grumbled.

He refused to lose his cool. "If you'll wait until I finish talking, you'll know."

"Fine. All right. I'm waiting...."

He drew in a slow breath and continued, "The party ended. I kept drinking. Eventually I passed out on this dirt road, still up in the mountains. Don't know how I got on that road or when I just fell down and didn't get up. But that was when I got the help I badly needed. It was on that road that the guy who changed my life found me. His name was Wily Dunn."

"He found you passed out in the middle of the road?"

"That's about the size of it. He took me home, helped me to quit drinking and get back on my feet. In time, he let me work for him. I learned fast. Turned out I had a knack for working with wood."

"So you're saying *you* work for *him*."

"I did. Until last November. He died. And he left his company, Dunn Woodworkers, to me—he left everything to me." He waited for her to say something to that. She only glared. So he prompted, "Does that explain it clearly enough for you?" Her answer was a surly little shrug. But he refused to give up. "So while I'm here, I'd like to use your workshop if you'll let me. But the main thing is that it would be better, as far as getting to know Johnny, if I lived closer than I would be if I stayed at the Sierra Star."

She spoke then. Finally. "You really think you need to be closer than down the street?"

"I want to be…around. So he sees me all the time."

"You can be around and stay down the street."

"It's not the same. If I'm staying here, he'll see me several times a day. And I won't have to knock on the front door just to talk to him. I'll be in and out of the house."

She closed her eyes, let out a heavy sigh and then forced herself to look at him again. "You mean you want to eat with us."

"If that's okay, yeah. And I can wash up and shave mostly at the trough by the side of the barn."

"Oh, come on, get real. I shut off the outside faucets before the first hard freeze. At the very least, you'll need hot water and a toilet."

"Yeah, well. I can use the downstairs bathroom. It's near the back door, so I won't have to be trooping through your house. And it's got a shower."

"So you'll need to be in the house several times a day—to eat breakfast, lunch and dinner *and* every time you need the use of a bathroom."

"Glory, come on. I'll stay out of your way as much as possible. And I could…help out around the house, clean up the yard if it needs it, fix whatever's broken. And fill in at the hardware store, too, if you need someone there while you're recovering. I know it's a lot to ask...."

"It's more than a lot, Bowie. It's too much to ask. Basically, you want to stay here, at my house, for an indefinite period of time. Just admit it."

He did want to stay there, yeah. And he didn't know yet for how long. Coaxingly, he tried again. "Look at it this way, the more time I can spend with Johnny day by day, the less time it will take overall."

"The less time it will take for what?"

"To get to know him. To...work things out with him. To make him see that I'm here now, in his life. That I won't go away again."

She scanned his face as though determined to ferret out darker motives. "Get straight with me, Bowie."

"I am being straight with you."

"Hah. What are you planning, really?"

"I just told you."

"I will tell you right now that if you think you can take him from me, you are very much mistaken."

That was too much. "Stop it." He spoke with more heat than he'd allowed himself up until then. "That is not what I'm here for."

"You just said—"

"I meant that I won't...disappear again, that I'll be available for him whenever he needs me."

She made a scoffing sound. "You're ready for that? Really? To stick with him, to be a part of his life, no matter how rough it gets?"

"I am. Yes."

"If you...make him love you. And then you leave him..." A sheen of tears made her brown eyes glitter. She looked away.

He felt like a complete jerk, which, if you came right

down to it, he had been for a lot of his life. He waited until she faced him again before he vowed, "I won't do that, Glory. I won't desert him again. Not ever. No matter what."

Her mouth was quivering. Sera fussed at her breast. "Turn away," she commanded in a torn whisper.

He went back to the window. Sera let out more fussy little sounds and he heard the box springs shift.

"All right," Glory said. He turned and took a few steps toward the bed. She had Sera at her other breast now. And the tears were gone from her big brown eyes. She tipped her head to the side, gave him another slow once-over. Finally, she spoke. "There couldn't be any drinking, do you understand?"

Relief poured through him, sweet and cool as water from a mountain spring. She was going to go for it, going to let him stay. "There won't be," he promised solemnly.

"And no fighting."

"Never. I'm done with all that crap. I give you my word."

She glared at him, those dark eyes flashing fire. And suddenly, he was remembering their first time together. In his room in the attic at the Sierra Star.

She'd been working as a maid for his mom, living in a room downstairs....

And she had chased him, from the first day she started working at the B and B. She'd flashed those famous Dellazola dimples at him every time he looked her way and she always found reasons to stop working and visit with him every chance she got.

He'd tried to do the right thing, although the right thing was never his strong suit. For months, he'd avoided her. She was only nineteen and he was five years older, too old for her, he'd thought. Especially given that he drank too much and he got in fights, that every job he'd ever had, he'd managed to get himself fired from.

And then, well, he'd known her practically since she was born, watched her grow from a skinny, loud, bossy little kid. She was the baby of her family and she'd learned early that when you were a Dellazola, you had to make a lot of noise if you hoped to get your share of the attention. He'd always thought she was cute, but still, it seemed wrong to give her what she wanted from him.

Once she started at the B and B and he was around her a lot more, he couldn't help but finally see her as a woman, see how fine she was, gutsy and smart and full of fire. He'd felt the attraction definitely. But he'd promised himself he wouldn't give in to it.

Now, there was a promise he was born to break.

Finally, she came to his room on a cool spring night, all dressed for bed in a little white nightie. She'd tapped on his door and slipped inside before he even had a chance to tell her to go away.

And then she stood in front of the lamp. She knew exactly what she was doing. He could see right through that little nightie of hers and what he saw made him groan out loud.

He said no. Twice.

But as soon as she threw herself into his arms, he was a goner. She smelled like rain and apples, all fresh and sweet and clean. And her mouth was under his, those soft, wide lips opening to invite his tongue inside....

She stayed with him until just before dawn, when she tiptoed back down the stairs to her own room. After that, she came to him every night. He was the happiest man alive. He even gave up the drinking and the fighting.

For a while, anyway. But eventually, his troublesome nature got the better of him. He came home drunk now and then. He got in a few fights. He knew he was a disappointment to her, and that only seemed to make him drink more and stay out all night and come home in the morning bruised and battered from some brawl he couldn't even remember being part of.

It only got worse when she found out she was pregnant and refused to marry him....

"Don't you tell me any of your lies, Bowie Bravo." Her low, angry words snapped him back to the here and now.

He faced her squarely. "I'm not lying. I did a lot of things wrong, made a lot of bad choices. But I never lied to you and you know that."

"You never lied to me? What about all those times you promised to quit drinking, to stop fighting, to get a job and keep it?"

She was right. Faintly, he heard Wily's wry voice in his head. *The truth may not set you free, son. But it's a start.*

He made himself bust to it. "Okay, you got me there. When it came to the drinking, I had no control. I lied when I was drinking—to you, to Ma, to everyone I cared about. To myself, most of all. But I'm not drinking now. And I am telling you honestly that I don't want to take Johnny away from you. That would be wrong and I really am trying to do the right thing here. I only want to find a way to be a father to him, like I should have been all along."

She stared up at him for a long time, cradling her baby's head so gently against her breast. Finally, she asked in a ragged little whisper, "You mean that?"

He didn't let his gaze waver. "I swear it, Glory."

"Fine. Take the workshop. It's yours."

Chapter Five

"He's had a phone installed out there in Matteo's workshop," Glory said, leaning close across the table so only Angie would hear. "And cable, too, for his fancy computer."

It was one week after Sera's birth and Glory's first time out of the house. With Sera all bundled up in the stroller, she'd walked from her house to Dixie's Diner on Main Street and met Angie for lunch. It was cold out, but at least the winter sun was shining. What remained of the snow from the big storm the previous Monday was piled in dirty mounds along the sides of the streets.

Angie sipped her iced tea. They always had iced tea when they met at the diner for lunch, no matter what time of year it was. It was kind of a tradition with them. Angie asked, "But…it's working out all right, isn't it?"

Glory made a humphing sound. "He also had a lot of equipment delivered…tools and fancy saws and stuff."

"Well, Glory, if he's going to work, he's going to need the tools to do it with."

"I know that." She sounded snappish to her own ears and made an effort to gentle her tone. "It's just…oh, I don't know. He's been great, really. Fine."

"So he hasn't been out drinking and brawling till all hours?"

"He swore he wouldn't. And he's kept his word for a whole week." She piled on the sarcasm. "I am so impressed."

Angie kept after her. "He cooks breakfast for you and Johnny every morning, right? And he fixed that leaky faucet in the downstairs bathroom."

Glory nodded grudgingly. "Yeah, and if there's a problem at the store, he hustles right over there to handle it, follows my instructions to the letter. I swear I can't leave unfolded laundry in the laundry room. When I go back to deal with it, it's all in neat little stacks."

Angie laughed. "It's what I said yesterday, the last time we talked about this. He sounds like the perfect man to me."

"Not funny," Glory said bleakly. "Not funny at all."

"Johnny warming up to him any yet?"

Glory shook her head. "Only speaks to him when spoken to. Avoids him if at all possible."

"Give him time."

"Yeah, right." She bent over the stroller, which she'd parked at the side of the booth, and smiled at her baby, who was lying there quietly for once, waving her tiny hands and making soft cooing sounds. "What a good girl you're being," she said indulgently. And then she sat up straight and faced her sister again. "Johnny won't give him the time of day. But Sera…"

"Yeah?"

"Adores him. I'm not kidding. He's magic with her. She's not like Johnny was. She's colicky and fussy a lot of the time—well, you know that." She waited for Angie's nod of confirmation before she continued, "All he has to do is hold her in those big arms of his and she coos and giggles and acts like a perfect little angel."

Angie swallowed a bite of BLT and whispered, teasingly, "So, Glory, just how big *are* Bowie's arms?"

Glory dredged a french fry in ketchup and stuck it in her mouth. "Please, don't."

But Angie had no mercy. Not about this. "You've still got it bad for him. I can see it in your eyes."

"Oh, God, you're saying I'm that obvious?"

Angie shook her head. "Uh-uh. *I* can see it. But I know you better than just about anyone. Everyone one else thinks you're barely tolerating him."

"Good."

"Mamma says you really ought to be nicer to the poor guy. And then Aunt Stella quotes scripture about how a woman ought to be gentle and forgiving—and you're not."

"Mamma and Aunt Stella can just mind their own damn business."

Angie chuckled. "Yeah, like that's gonna happen."

Glory knew she was a fortunate woman to have a sister she could trust absolutely with even her most shameful secrets. She ate another french fry, and then leaned across the booth again and spoke very softly. "He's always been my big, bad weakness. When I think of the way I chased him way back at the beginning…"

"You were crazy about him and you were young. It's hardly a crime that you went after what you wanted."

"Well, I'm not so young now."

"Oh, stop it. You're not even thirty."

"Sometimes I *feel* old."

Angie's shrug was philosophical. "Don't we all?"

"And you'd think at least I would have gotten a little smarter over the years, huh? Especially after Matteo, after I finally learned all it *can* be, between a man and a woman...."

"You feel what you feel. Don't be so hard on yourself."

"Easy for you to say. You've got Brett. He's as good a husband as Matteo was *and* as hot as Bowie."

Angie arched an eyebrow. "So Matteo wasn't hot?"

"Of course he was. You know what I meant."

"And *you* know that Brett and I have had our issues."

"Yeah, and you worked through them. Brett didn't just vanish from your life—and then never bother to come back."

"Bowie came back. And at the right time, too, considering that he was the only one there to lend a hand when Sera was born."

Glory let out a humorless laugh. "You're my sister, remember? You're supposed to be on *my* side."

"Just keeping you honest."

"Oh, right. It's for my own good that you keep pointing out all the crap I don't even want to admit to myself."

"Yep, that's about the size of it."

Glory leaned close again. "You don't understand. It's... humiliating to feel this way about him after the way he left us cold for all those years."

"People change, Glory. It's obvious to everyone that Bowie has changed."

"Yeah, well, I don't care. He's not getting close to me again, not getting a chance to break my heart a second time."

"Does he know you've still got feelings for him?"

Glory sucked in an angry gasp. "He does not. And he will not. I get that it's the right thing, to let him have his chance with Johnny. I get that my son needs to make his peace with his natural father. So I'm doing my bit to make that happen. But if he screws up this time, if he abandons my boy again, well, I'm going to make his life a misery. Just see if I don't."

Angie shook a French fry at her. "Gee, Glory, don't go being too open-minded about all this."

Glory made a snarling sound and tucked into her BLT.

A few minutes later, Charlene, the owner of the diner and also Brand Bravo's wife, came by the booth to say hi. Charlene had blond hair and blue eyes and she was six months pregnant with her and Brand's first baby. They already had one child at home, though. They'd raised six-year-old Mia, who was Charlene's younger sister's daughter, since Mia was only a few weeks old.

Charlene refilled their iced teas, set the pitcher on the table and bent over the stroller. "Most gorgeous little girl I ever saw—well, next to our Mia, of course."

Glory beamed. "You want to hold her?"

"Do the robins show up in the spring?" Charlene reached out eager arms and scooped Sera up out of the stroller. She cradled her bobbly little head against her shoulder and cooed at her tenderly. "Oh, aren't you the sweetest thing?"

The usually fussy Sera laid her cheek against Charlene and looked around the diner with wide eyes as though she'd never seen such marvels as a long, Formica-topped counter and chrome stools with red vinyl seats—and come to think of it, she hadn't because this was her first time outside of the house.

Charlene swayed gently from side to side, rocking the baby. "Oh, I want one just like you," she said. Then, with some reluctance, she bent and put her back in the stroller and picked up the pitcher of tea. "This Saturday," she said to both Angie and Glory, "dinner up at our house. Say, six o'clock? Bring the kids." She grinned at Angie. "And my brother-in-law, too."

"Will do," Angie promised. "Can't wait."

"I called Chastity last night and invited her," Charlene said. "And Bowie came by for lunch yesterday. I asked him to come. He said he'd be there."

Glory kept her smile in place. "Great." After all, Bowie *was* Charlene's brother-in-law. Of course Charlene would invite him. She said, "Johnny and Sera and I would love to come. What can we bring?"

"Just yourselves—and that means you, too, Angie. Don't bring a thing. You both could use a night off from cooking, I'll bet."

"Oh, yeah," said Glory.

"Can we ever," Angie agreed.

"See you Saturday." Charlene carried the pitcher back behind the counter and picked up the coffeepot. She got to work filling empty cups.

Angie let out a big, fake sigh. "Saturday dinner with the Bravo boys, Bowie included…"

"Do you have to rub it in?"

"Keep smilin'," Angie teased.

"Oh, I will. Just you watch me."

In the barn behind Glory's house, Bowie wrapped up a video conference with his office at the Santa Cruz workshop. He sat back in the old easy chair and felt pretty good about how the business was getting along in his absence.

The jobs in progress were all on schedule. He had good people and he paid them well. They did fine work. And the few top customers who expected him to build their stuff personally were willing to wait for him to have the time to give them.

The tools and equipment he'd ordered so he could work while he was in the Flat had already arrived. Within the next few days he'd be receiving a shipment of good red oak reclaimed from a collapsed South Carolina grist mill. That mill had stood for well over a hundred years. Bowie would use the old, weathered boards to make a dining-room table and chairs, as well as a bedroom suite for a client who was building a house in Salem, Oregon. Bowie was looking forward to getting started on that project.

In the meantime, he'd brought some bits of old bass-wood with him. He whittled as a hobby and basswood was about the best wood there was for a whittler. It was soft and yet not prone to splitting. He picked up the piece he'd sketched out the evening before and he grabbed his bench knife—a plain, serviceable knife with a fixed single blade and a wooden handle. He started whittling away at it, working to shave off the wood along the lines he'd drawn.

As he worked at the bit of wood, he thought about what *wasn't* going so well.

Johnny. And Glory, too. Glory treated him civilly, but never with anything resembling warmth or friendliness. At this rate, making peace with her was never going to happen. He had hoped by the time he was ready to leave town again that he and Glory would be on good terms.

And Johnny? The boy never said a word to Bowie unless Bowie spoke to him first. And, except at mealtime, he very rarely hung around if Bowie was in the room.

Sometimes, in the past couple of days, he'd caught the kid watching him. Johnny always turned away so fast that Bowie couldn't tell if the boy was looking at him with hostility or curiosity—or maybe even something resembling interest. Bowie told himself to consider the boy's furtive glances as progress.

Did he believe that? Not really.

Bowie set the bit of basswood aside and put his knife away. It was lunchtime. Johnny was in school. He had no idea what Glory might be doing. Seemed a good time to get out for a while, maybe stop at Dixie's Diner, say hi to Charlene and enjoy a big bowl of her famous chili smothered in cheddar and onions.

Funny how things change, he thought as he strolled down the street from Upper Main. People waved and smiled at him. That had surprised him the first few days. He'd expected a lot of scowls and disapproving glances.

But he'd been gone quite a while. And so far, he hadn't made trouble for anyone, hadn't drunk himself into a stupor or beat anyone's face in. Folks seemed willing to accept him and treat him with kindness. Maybe they saw that he'd grown up a little in the time he was away. Maybe they were willing to give him a chance, to see how he acted before they judged him—unlike a certain dimpled brunette he could mention but wouldn't. Because he wasn't thinking about her now. He was just walking down the street in his old hometown under the washed-out winter sun, on his way to the diner for lunch.

"Bowie! Man, I heard you were back in town. How you been?" A tall, wasted-looking dude with his long graying hair tied back with a strip of leather and a couple of teeth missing in front came at him from the St. Thomas Bar across the street.

Bowie smiled and wished he could remember the guy's name. Someone he used to get drunk with, no doubt. "Hey." He held out his hand and they shook. The guy clapped him on the back and as he did it, the name came. "Zeb. Zeb Bickman." Bowie seemed to remember a couple of brawls he and Zeb had gotten into together. And maybe one fight, at least, where the two of them had been drunk on their asses and ended up on opposite sides. Details were fuzzy. As they generally were when he looked back on that time of his life.

"Come on across the street," Zeb lisped through his missing teeth. "Let me buy you a beer."

"I don't drink anymore."

"Hey. Well. Whatever works. A tall club soda, then?"

Bowie was past the point when he went into bars and ordered club soda to prove that he could. Mostly, being in bars just depressed him now. "Thanks, but no. I'm on my way to Charlene's place to get some lunch."

"Oh, man, you sure? You don't want to whet the ol' whistle for old time's sake?" Zeb waited for Bowie's shrug before adding, "'Nother time, then."

"You bet."

"Heard you were staying at the Rossi place."

"In the workshop out back, yeah." He didn't need Zeb getting the wrong idea, thinking he was living with Glory or anything like that.

"Heard you delivered Glory's little girl."

"I did, yeah."

"Whoa. Delivering a kid is a messy job that ought to be left to the professionals, if you ask me."

"It turned out all right. That's what matters." He reminded himself not to get testy with Zeb for being all up in his business. It was just that way in the Flat. Everybody knew everything about everyone.

But then Zeb's smile twisted into a leer. "She's still hotter than a firecracker, that Glory. Went and married that solid citizen mamma's boy, Matteo Rossi, though. Bet that chapped your ass, huh?"

Bowie got that feeling. Like ants chewing under his skin. He didn't do anything about it, though. He only looked steadily at Zeb—and thought about knocking out a few more of his teeth. The fact that he just thought about it was the difference between who he had been and who he was now.

Apparently, Zeb read Bowie's expression correctly. He put up both hands. "Hey, seriously, man, no offense meant."

"None taken," Bowie lied. "Gotta go. You take care of yourself now, Zeb."

Zeb was already backing away into the middle of the street. "Yeah, you bet. See you around, man."

Bowie started walking again, doubtful that Zeb would be offering to buy him any more tall club sodas.

Which was a-okay with him.

He crossed Commerce Lane and went on down past the old theater and a couple of shops. On the other side of the street, Old Tony Dellazola, Glory's great-granddad, sat on a bench in front of the grocery store. He raised his hand in a wave. Bowie waved back. Two gray-haired women came out of the diner as he approached the glass-topped door. A couple of nice, churchgoing ladies. In days gone by, they would have granted him a wary frown at best.

They smiled at him and nodded.

He nodded back. "Ladies…" He caught the door and went in.

He spotted Sera's stroller first, by a booth near the back wall—and then he saw Glory. She was sitting with Angie, who gave him a wave. Glory spotted him, too. She pinched up her mouth and then looked away fast.

What? He should have somehow known she would be here and stayed away today?

To hell with that. If she didn't want him in the diner at the same time as she was, she'd damn well have to tell him when she was going and that she didn't want to see him there. From back in the barn, he couldn't see when she left the house. And it wasn't his business anyway to keep track of her comings and goings.

"Bowie, hi." Brand's wife greeted him with a big smile.

He took a stool at the counter, ordered his chili and flipped his coffee cup up so that Charlene could fill it. She turned to stick his order on the wheel.

And Sera started fussing. It began with a couple of questioning little cries, and within about sixty seconds had escalated to a full-out wail.

In the corner of his eye, he watched Glory take her out of the stroller. She patted her back and tried to calm her. Nursing would probably quiet her, but Glory didn't try that. Maybe she felt uncomfortable about nursing in public.

The pleasant hum of conversation in the place had ceased. There was only Sera, yowling as though she would never stop.

Sera wailed on as Bowie slid off the stool and went to the booth. When he got there, Glory didn't even say a word. She gave him a dirty look and passed him the crying baby.

He cradled her close and whispered, "Shh, now. It's okay."

She made the cutest little sound, a cry that ended with a contented sigh. And then she laid her head down on his shoulder. He patted her tiny little back and kind of wished he could just hold on to her forever. "Okay if I just rock her a minute or two?" he asked Glory.

She glared up at him. With Sera quiet, the diner was dead silent now. Everyone in the place seemed to be watching to see if spunky Glory Dellazola Rossi was about to give troublesome Bowie Bravo what for.

But she only gritted her teeth and made herself smile. "Thanks, Bowie. You go right ahead." Across the table from her, Angie was grinning. Glory sent her sister an evil glance and Angie wiped that grin right off her face.

Bowie carried Sera back to the counter. After a minute or two, the buzz of different conversations started up again.

Charlene put his chili in front of him and rested her hand on the top of her round stomach, the way pregnant women do. "Looks like you got a way with babies," she said.

He made sure that Sera was resting securely against him and then used his free hand to pick up his spoon. "Just this one. She and I understand each other."

"How's that?" asked the old guy on the stool next to him.

He answered loud enough that Glory probably heard him if she happened to be listening. "I'm only here to help. Sera here, she gets that."

Glory *had* heard what Bowie said at the diner.

And for the rest of the day, it did kind of nag at her— okay, more than kind of. It nagged at her a lot.

Because he really did seem to be there to help. And maybe, as Angie had more or less told her to her face, she needed to lighten up a little with him.

Yeah, there was the problem that she was still attracted to him when she knew she shouldn't be. But, come on, what kind of problem was that if he didn't feel the same way? Because he didn't. She knew that. If he did, he would have given her some kind of sign by now.

Wouldn't he?

Oh, for crying out loud, what did it matter if he did or didn't still have any interest in her as a woman? She'd just had a baby. Sex ought to be the last thing on her mind.

What she ought to be concerned about was helping

her son and his father find some kind of peace with each other. And she knew she wasn't doing that. On the contrary, it was more than possible that her hostility toward Bowie was giving Johnny the excuse he needed not to let Bowie get too close.

It was even possible that Johnny was taking his cues from her when it came to Bowie. With the kind of signals she was sending, Johnny could very well be thinking that he would not only be disloyal to Matteo's memory if he got to know his biological father, but disloyal to her, to Glory, as well.

Maybe she needed to…lead the way a little for him. She needed to put aside her own issues with Bowie, to make it clear to Johnny that she thought Bowie was okay, so that Johnny could give himself permission to do the same.

That night at dinner, it was just the three of them. Glory made a point to be nicer to Bowie. She even made herself smile at him. Twice.

The first time she smiled, Bowie was passing her the butter. He blinked and almost dropped the butter dish. She stifled a nervous laugh and caught the dish just in time.

"Thank you," she said as pleasantly as she could manage.

"Uh, you're welcome," he answered in a stunned sort of tone.

Out of the corner of her eye, she could see Johnny watching them. Good.

The second time she smiled at Bowie was when he got right up and started clearing off the table when the meal was done. And she went beyond just the smile that time. She even said, "Bowie, I do appreciate your helping out the way you do."

Bowie slid her a look. "Happy to," he answered gruffly.

Johnny said, "Can I go watch the Disney Channel for an hour?"

"Help Bowie clear the table," she instructed.

He was a good kid, always had been. He got up and went to work. The clearing-off was done in record time.

"Disney?" Johnny tried again.

"Homework?" she quizzed.

"Done, Mom. You know that."

"One hour," she finally agreed.

He shot out of that kitchen faster than a cat with its tail on fire. She heard the TV start up in the other room.

Bowie was standing at the counter, watching her. She considered giving him a third smile. But Johnny wasn't there to see it and why go overboard? She got up and went to the sink and started loading the dishwasher. "I heard what you said in the diner today—about only being here to help."

He leaned back against the counter a few feet away and folded his arms over that broad chest of his. "I was just thinking that probably you had."

She made herself throw in a little more praise. "And you *have* been helpful. You really have." After all, it was only the truth.

"You're welcome. Not that it makes any difference to him." Bowie tipped his head in the direction of the family room.

She loaded in the last plate and pulled the top rack out to put in the glassware. "Give him time."

"It's been a week."

"A week is nothing. Think how long you've been gone." As soon as the words were out, she realized they sounded disapproving.

He braced his hands on the counter behind him, and glanced off toward the far wall. "I do think about it, Glory. All the time."

She tried again. "I didn't mean to be critical. It just... came out that way."

He sent her a look from those summer-blue eyes. "Have you noticed that most of what you say to me 'just comes out that way'?"

She pushed the top rack in, bent and shut the dishwasher door. And then she grabbed a towel and dried her hands. "All right, I get that. I'll...make a point not to give you such a bad time from now on."

"That would be good. Really good."

"And how about if I send Johnny out to you to say good-night—you know, before he goes to bed?"

His slow smile did something scary to her heartstrings. "I would really appreciate that." The smile vanished. "Not that he would come."

"Hey," she softly advised, "don't predict the worst, okay?"

"You're right. This is hard enough with a *good* attitude."

She laughed. "That's the spirit." Right then, the monitor on the sideboard erupted with fussy little whines.

They were both silent, waiting. Sometimes Sera would whimper a little and go back to sleep.

But she didn't. The fussing got louder until it became out-and-out wailing.

Bowie offered, "Want me to get her?" He looked hopeful.

Glory wasn't sure how she felt about the way he was with Sera. Until now, she'd just been resentful—of his presence in her house, of the way her newborn daughter had taken to him instantly and unconditionally. Because of what had happened in the past, she'd felt justified in her resentment. He'd been ready and willing to comfort her daughter from the very moment Sera was born. And yet Glory could count on one hand the number of times he'd held his own baby son in his arms. Also, it didn't seem right that Matteo's child seemed to like troublemaking Bowie Bravo more than she liked her own mother.

Lighten up, Glory, she told herself. Again. "Sure, go get her. That would be great."

He turned and left the kitchen faster than Johnny had when she told him he could spend an hour with the Disney Channel.

Progress.

Bowie thought the word and smiled.

It was later that night and he was out in the workshop, whittling away at his nice bit of basswood with a cozy fire going in the old parlor-style stove.

He really was making progress. With Glory, at least. She'd been great during dinner. And with a little luck, her new attitude might even rub off on Johnny.

Bowie set down his knife and sent a glance at the windup alarm clock on the rough pine shelf above the cot. It was after seven-thirty. She usually had Johnny in bed by eight or so, didn't she? Did that mean he wasn't coming after all?

And if he wasn't coming, was it because Glory hadn't kept her word about sending him to say good-night? Or because when she asked him to, he'd refused?

Bowie picked up the knife again and started working away at the wood. He shook his head as he whittled, feeling all nervous and edgy. Hoping the kid would come, afraid that he wouldn't. Seriously, he needed to get hold of himself.

What will happen, will happen, Wily would say. *A man can help things along by taking action. But wishin' and hopin' never did make a single dream come true.*

Bowie looked at the clock again. Seven-thirty-eight. His stomach was tied in knots and his heart was a ball of lead in his chest.

And then he heard the hesitant tap on the workshop door.

His lead ball of a heart leaped to bouncing life. And he longed to jump to his feet and throw open the door.

But instead, he forced himself to keep his eyes on his whittling. "It's open," he called in an easy voice that completely belied the churning excitement within him.

He did look up then, wood and knife all but forgotten in his hands as the door slowly opened. Johnny was on the other side, wearing his winter jacket, a wool hat and flannel airplane pajamas tucked into his rubber boots. His dark eyes were steady and serious. An icy gust of wind blew in around him.

Bowie gave him a couple of seconds to say something. When he didn't, Bowie went for it. "Come on in. Shut the door. It's freezing out there."

Johnny did as he was told, stepping inside and turning to push the door carefully closed until the latch clicked. After that, he simply stood there, with his back against the door, wearing an expression that said he'd rather be just about anywhere else.

Bowie said, "You can hang your coat on that peg there." He pointed with his roughed-out piece of basswood.

"It's okay." The boy didn't move. His hair was still wet from his bath, slicked down close to his head. Bowie would have bet good money that he smelled of soap and toothpaste, but he doubted the kid would get close enough for him to know for sure.

Bowie lowered his head and went to work again, putting his concentration on the small job between his hands, telling himself that he wasn't going to push. Not now. If he looked up and Johnny was gone, well, so be it. There would be other bedtimes.

This wasn't his only chance. Even if it felt like it.

One step. Two. In his peripheral vision, Bowie could see Johnny's rubber boots. *Come on. It's okay. ...*

There. No doubt. The smell of toothpaste.

"What are you making?" Johnny asked.

"A train set." Bowie kept shaving away at the wood.

Johnny was maybe three feet from Bowie's chair. "You mean a *whole* train set, with cars and an engine, a caboose and everything, all out of wood?"

"Yes, that's what I mean."

"That's a funny-looking knife. What kind of knife is that?" Johnny reached out a hand.

Bowie sent him a warning glance. "Don't touch it. It's very sharp. It's called a bench knife." He held the knife up—but out of the way. "Nice rounded wooden handle, a short, stable blade, tapered so that the tip can get into tight spaces, but wide at the base, so it's strong enough for heavy cuts...."

Johnny's eyes kind of glazed over. Bowie almost grinned. Okay, the wonders of his bench knife were a little over the head of a six-year-old.

But a train set sure wasn't. "How many cars?" Johnny asked.

"Well, I think at least ten. More, if I feel ambitious."

"More than ten." Eyes wide as saucers. "Will you paint it and everything?"

"I sure will."

"That would be good."

"I'll remember you said that."

"Who will it be for—I mean, when it's finished?"

Bowie set his knife on the table by his chair and reached for the mug of coffee he'd mixed up a while ago using the water he kept going on the stove and a jar of instant he'd picked up at the grocery store yesterday. He sipped, trying to think how to tell Johnny it was for him without making some big deal of it.

But he never got a chance to say the words he was so carefully choosing. In the split second he had glanced away, Johnny had reached for the knife.

He must have got it by the blade.

Out of nowhere, blood was spurting.

And Johnny dropped the knife to the floor and let loose with a long, loud, terrified scream.

Chapter Six

In the kitchen, Glory heard Johnny scream. She flew out the back door and raced for the barn, shoving back the door to the workshop so hard that it banged against a workbench, rattling a bunch of tools hanging on a pegboard above.

She saw Johnny by the stove, holding his right wrist with his left hand. Blood poured from right palm. He turned and looked at her. "Mom," he said. He seemed calm now. There had been only that one terrible shriek. "I cut myself...."

Glory wanted to run to him, but something held her back. Maybe that he seemed so calm. If she got all over him, he would only get upset again.

Plus, Bowie was there, beside him, with a white T-shirt in his hands. As she watched, Bowie ripped a strip off the shirt and wrapped it quickly—and tightly—around the wound.

"Make a fist of your hand and hold it up," Bowie said, "over your head...."

Johnny's T-shirt-wrapped fist shot into the air. "This way?"

"That's it. Just right. The blood doesn't pump so hard when you keep the wound up above your heart."

"Above my heart," Johnny repeated in a dazed and wondering tone.

Bowie, as calm as their son—and even more white around the mouth—spoke to her then. "I'm guessing he'll need some stitches. We should call Brett...."

"I'm on it." She turned.

"There's a phone here," he said.

But she was already dashing back the way she'd come. The truth was, her mind had gone blank. She couldn't remember her own sister's number. And in the house, she had it on auto dial. She grabbed the phone the minute she was back inside, hit the right button for Angie's house.

Brett answered. "Bravo residence."

In a breathless rush, she told him that Johnny had cut his hand and probably needed stitches.

"Wrap it tight and keep it elevated," he said.

"Done."

"Good. Bring him over to the clinic, then. I'll meet you there."

She hung up and whirled to run back to the barn. But Bowie and Johnny, with his small, bloody fist high, were already coming up the back-porch steps. She held the door open for them. "Brett says he'll meet us at the clinic."

Bowie asked, "Sera asleep?"

"I'll just get her." Glory started to whirl away again, this time for the stairs.

He caught her arm. "Wait." She froze—and blinked down at the sight of his big, warm hand wrapped around her elbow. He let go instantly. "I just mean, why wake her up?" he asked carefully. "I can take him—or stay here with her and you can go."

Johnny gazed up at Bowie. "We should go," he said gravely, his fist still up in the air. "Mom can watch Sera."

Glory wanted to burst into tears. Her son needed stitches and he hadn't once cried or clung to her. Plus, he had actually volunteered to let Bowie take him.

She was happy about that—or at least, she knew it for the breakthrough it was. He was a great kid. And it looked like he might actually begin to forge a relationship with his father, after all.

Still, her mother's heart ached. He was growing up so fast. She'd never realized—how swiftly it was all going to happen, how quickly he would grow up and start to claim his independence, a state that set him apart from her.

Bowie, still way too white around the mouth and grim around the eyes, deferred to her. "Glory?"

She made herself nod. "Yeah, you two go on. I'll stay with Sera."

Now he looked doubtful—or maybe more like scared to death. "You sure?"

"Come *on,* Bowie," Johnny insisted. He actually got hold of Bowie's sleeve with his uninjured hand and gave it a tug. "I need to see Uncle Brett right now. 'Cause I need *stitches.*"

Bowie seemed to shake himself. "All right, let's get going." He fumbled in the pocket of the jacket he must have thrown on when she ran for the phone. The keys jingled in his hand.

Johnny was already headed for the front door, rubber boots clump, clump, clumping past the stairs. Bowie sent her a last, desperate glance over his shoulder as he went after him.

The front door opened. And then it shut. A minute later, she heard Bowie's SUV start up outside.

She put her hand against her aching heart and whispered, "Drive carefully," even though they were already gone.

The lights were on at the clinic when Bowie pulled into a parking space in front.

In the backseat, Johnny barely waited for the car to stop moving before popping the latch on his seat belt and jumping out. Injured hand still held high, he raced up the steps and grabbed the doorknob with his good hand. It was open.

Johnny threw the door wide, "Uncle Brett! I'm here and it looks like I'm gonna need stitches!"

Brett called, "Back here, Johnny!"

Johnny bolted across the reception area to the open doorway that led to the exam rooms. Bowie followed, hating himself for what had happened.

The lights were on in the first exam room. Brett signaled them in. "So, what's happened here?"

The blood—so dark, so red, so much of it—had soaked through the torn section of T-shirt. Bowie felt sick every time he looked at it.

Johnny waved his bloody fist triumphantly. "Bowie told me not to touch the knife, but I touched the knife." Now he looked at Brett with serious eyes. "Uncle Brett, it was *very* sharp."

Brett sent a glance at Bowie and Bowie saw the glint of humor in his brother's eyes. What was so funny? Not a thing, the way Bowie saw it. The kid could have bled to death. And Bowie knew whose fault that would have been.

"Let's have a look." Brett snapped on exam gloves.

"Can you take off that jacket and get up on the bench by yourself?"

Johnny got the jacket off without much trouble. "Here, Bowie."

Bowie stepped up to take the jacket. There was blood on the sleeve. And also on the sleeve and down the front of his airplane pajamas. Bowie felt sick at the sight. All that blood. And now the poor kid would need his hand sewn up. Why? Because his long-lost, would-be dad didn't have sense enough to keep a sharp knife out of his reach.

At least Johnny was taking it all in stride. He proudly got on the stool and clambered onto the examining bench. "Will I have to have a *shot?* Bobby Winkle had a shot that time he had those stitches in his knee. Remember that, Uncle Brett?"

"Yes, I do." Brett swung a steel tray on a stand in front of Johnny. "Okay, put your hand here."

"Below my *heart?*"

"I think we're safe to try that now. The bleeding seems to have slowed a little." Johnny held out his hand and Brett unwrapped the bloody strip of cloth. "Okay, now, this might sting." He went to work cleaning the gash.

Johnny was a trouper. He shut his eyes tight and tipped his head back. And said "ow" only twice. After the cleaning, it was time for that shot Johnny had asked about.

"This will numb the area." Brett delivered the injection smoothly, with little fanfare.

Bowie couldn't bear to watch. He stuck his hands in his pockets and looked away and hated himself some more. Johnny whimpered when the needle went in but quickly regained his composure.

And his excitement. He watched, fascinated, as Brett

stitched him up. "Wow, nine stitches. That's a lot, huh, Uncle Brett?"

Brett bandaged him up. "Yes, it is. And you shouldn't have touched that knife."

"I know. I was bad." The big brown eyes turned Bowie's way. "I'm sorry, Bowie." Bowie gave him a nod.

Brett said, "But as far as getting the stitches goes, you did very, very well."

Johnny's brown eyes shone. "I didn't cry once, did I?"

"Nope, not once."

"Do I get a tattoo?"

Brett snapped off his gloves, dropped them in the trash and grabbed a clear glass bowl from a shelf by the sink. "You get two."

Johnny proudly fished out two temporary tattoos. One of a skull and crossbones, the other of a yellow shield with SuperKid printed in red across it. "Thank you," he said.

Brett gave him a wink and turned to Bowie, who stood near the door again, wrapped up in his own personal hell, reliving that moment when Johnny screamed. "Don't disturb the bandage for forty-eight hours," Brett said. "Don't let him get it wet. After that, you can apply fresh antibiotic cream and a clean bandage. Children's acetaminophen or ibuprofen if he has any pain. He should come back in a week. If the area around the stitches gets red or swollen, give us a call."

Bowie gaped at his brother, the doctor. "Uh, gotcha," he said, thinking about those words *red or swollen.* What if the hand got infected? Bowie would never forgive himself.

Brett grinned and handed him a small folded pamphlet. "Instructions for care of the injury. Just in case you forget."

"Great."

"Nine stitches," Johnny crowed. "Bobby Winkle only got eight. Isn't that right, Uncle Brett?"

"That's right." Brett took him under the arms and swung him down from the examining bench. "Be careful with that hand, now."

"I will. I promise."

Glory was standing at the bay window in the family room, waiting for them, when Bowie's SUV pulled up in front of the house again. She watched as Johnny ran up the front walk, his right hand wrapped in a snow-white gauze bandage. Bowie followed after him at a more sedate pace.

As soon as her boy reached the porch, she went through the arch into the front hall so that she was waiting there when he pushed open the door.

"Mom!" He ran to her, arms outstretched. Her heart aching—but in a *good* way now—she gathered him in. "Mom, I had nine stitches! Nine! And Uncle Brett said I did very, very well."

She hugged him tighter. "Oh, you are a brave, brave boy."

Too soon, he was squirming to be free again. "I have to keep it clean and not get it wet and go back in a week."

She straightened to her height again. "It's all very exciting. Hang up your coat and take off your boots and maybe we should have a little hot chocolate before you go to bed…."

He was already easing his injured hand free of his coat sleeve, beaming up at her. "Hot chocolate. I think that's a good idea."

"And give me that coat." There was blood on the sleeve. "I'll soak it overnight. You'll have to wear your old coat tomorrow."

"'Kay." He handed it over.

She folded the jacket over her arm and glanced at Bowie, who stood by the door, his head hunched into his collar and his hands in his pockets. "A little hot chocolate, Bowie?"

"You know, if everything's all right now, I think I'll just go on out to the barn...."

Was something wrong? Yeah, it had been scary, but everything had worked out all right. Still, he didn't sound so good. She frowned at him.

But he was already focused on Johnny again. "Good night, Johnny."

Johnny was sitting on the bottom stair taking off his boots. "'Night."

"Care instructions—for his stitches," Bowie muttered, holding out a folded piece of paper. She took it from him. And then, without another word, he eased around her and headed for the kitchen. A moment later, she heard the back door open and close.

Johnny drank his hot chocolate and then went up to brush his teeth a second time. He was already in bed wearing clean pajamas when she went in to say goodnight.

He confessed in a solemn tone, "Bowie told me not to touch the knife, but I did. I told him I was sorry."

"Good." She smoothed his silky hair back off his forehead. "It all turned out okay, and I'm so glad about that. But what you did was wrong. Sharp things are not for kids."

"I know. I just wanted to hold it."

"If you wanted to hold it, you should have told Bowie. Then he would have either shown you the safe way to hold it, or explained why that wasn't a good idea."

"I *know,* Mom. It was dumb, what I did. I won't do that again."

"All right, then."

Reluctantly, he asked, "Will I have to have a big time-out and stay in my room after school for a whole month or something?"

"Hmm. Well, I don't think a time-out is necessary. I have a feeling you won't be grabbing any knife blades in the future."

"No, I will not," he vowed. "Never, not ever."

She bent and kissed his cheek. "Does your hand hurt?"

"A little. Maybe."

"I'll be right back." She went and got him a kids' ibu-profen and water.

He took the pill. "There." He passed the glass back to her. "I'll be just fine now, Mom. You don't have to worry."

"I'm so glad. Good night."

"'Night." He snuggled right down and shut his eyes.

She turned off the light, quietly shut the door—and right then, from the room next to Johnny's, she heard Sera fussing.

A half hour later, she had Sera fed, changed and back in her crib. Then she got Johnny's blood-spattered paja-mas out of the bathroom hamper and took them down-stairs to soak them with the jacket.

She ended up standing at the folding table, staring out the window above it at the barn.

The light was on in the workshop. She caught her lower lip between her teeth, worried it briefly and let it go with a sigh as she admitted to herself that she was concerned about Bowie.

He'd seemed so grim when he brought Johnny back from the visit with Brett. And he'd said no to hot chocolate—even though it would have meant a few more minutes with the son he was trying so hard to get closer to.

Something wasn't right.

Mind your own business, Glory. Just leave the guy alone. She needed to turn out the lights, lock the doors and go to bed. After all, she deserved every minute of sleep she could get. Sera would be awake again and making a racket in a couple of hours at the most.

But there was just something about that lonely light shining in the workshop window. She couldn't turn and walk away from that, not after she'd seen that lost, glum look on Bowie's face.

So she got her jacket and grabbed the baby monitor from the kitchen counter and went out the back door.

The last thing Bowie expected that night was a knock on the workshop door. He was sitting on the cot, his head in his hands when that knock came.

He dragged himself to his feet and went to answer. It was Glory, her arms wrapped around herself against the icy night air, clutching the baby monitor in one fist, her eyes very dark and troubled-looking. "What's up?" A terrible thought came to him and panic unleashed its claws. "Johnny?" He croaked the word.

"Relax," she said, and even put on a smile. "He's fine. Sound asleep. Mind if I come in?"

He stepped back and gestured her inside.

She hesitated. For a moment he thought she would simply turn and go back to the house, which would have been fine with him. Or so he tried to tell himself.

But then she moved forward. He shut the door behind her and then stayed there, back to the door, waiting for some word from her, some explanation as to why she'd come out here.

She set the monitor down and slowly circled the space, moving first to the working side of the room, stopping by the new table saw, pausing again at his lathe and yet again at his router table. "Got all your new tools ready to go?" she asked with an oblique glance. At his nod, she continued her slow circuit of the room. Finally, she stopped by the stove and held her hands out to warm them. "Cold out."

"Yeah," he said, still waiting. And still wondering what she had on her mind.

She took off her jacket and draped it over the back of an old wooden rocking chair. Finally, she gestured at the cot and the open duffel bag half-full of his clothes. "Planning a trip?"

Out of nowhere, he wanted a drink. Jack Black straight up. A double.

The desire shocked him a little. He'd come a long way from the days when he thought about drinking most of the time. Now, the hunger came infrequently.

And when it did, he recognized the sudden, sharp longing for what it was: a yen to escape something scary or difficult, a need to get away from a moment too painful to face.

He admitted, "Okay, Glory, yeah. I was thinking about leaving. About how maybe I shouldn't have come."

Her mouth pinched up. She glared at that duffel bag. "That bag tells me you were *more* than just thinking about it."

"Glory, come on..."

She whirled on him, brandy-brown eyes flashing, cheeks hot with color. "Don't you *'come on'* me, Bowie Bravo. What was your plan, then? To just take off, with no goodbyes and no explanations? Just disappear in the middle of the night?"

"No, that was not my plan." The words came out low and rough. Raw. "I...didn't have a plan, okay? I didn't know what the hell I was going to do. I only knew that Johnny wouldn't have nine stitches in his hand if it wasn't for me."

"How long were you planning to be gone this time, huh? Ten years? Twenty?"

"Stop it."

She came at him, fast, right arm raised. He was certain she was going to slap his face and he braced himself for the blow—but when she reached him, she only let out a low, furious growl through clenched teeth. "I would like to slap you silly about now."

"Got that. And go ahead. Be my guest."

She let her arm drop to her side. "And give you an excuse to make *me* the bad guy? No, thanks." She turned away, went to the rocking chair and plunked down into it. "Listen," she said, rocking furiously.

Like he had a choice. "What?"

She stopped in mid-rock. "You told me you were here to try and get to know Johnny, to be part of his life."

"That's right, but—"

She cut him off. "There are no buts when it comes to being a dad. No buts. You don't get to just take off because you feel *bad,* Bowie. Things go wrong and you know it's your fault, so what? You fix it the best you can and you work hard not to make the same mistake twice. And you keep on. Got it? You stick around, no matter what."

"Glory, I—"

She rolled right over him again. "Refresh my memory for me, will you?"

"It's just that—"

"I seem to recall that when I said you could stay here,

you promised you wouldn't go running off, no matter how tough things got. I seem to recall your swearing to me that you wouldn't desert Johnny again, no matter what."

"I know that. I—"

"Just tell me. Just say it. Did you make that promise or did you not?"

He sagged against the door. The woman exhausted him. She always had. "All right. Yeah, I made that promise."

"And do you intend to keep that promise?"

"I do, yes." He said it with feeling. Because it was true.

She scoffed and pointed. "That duffel bag over there tells me differently."

He straightened from the door. He was taller than her by more than a foot. And he had at least a hundred pounds of muscle and sinew over her. Yet somehow, she always seemed to know how to make him feel like something small and slimy that had just slithered out from under the nearest rock.

So what if she happened to be absolutely right in what she'd just said to him? Her rightness didn't take any of the sting out of her harsh words.

"Well," she prodded, sitting forward in the rocker, gripping the arms. "What do you have to say for yourself?"

He grunted. "You know, you always did have the knack of making me feel about two inches tall."

"Are you leaving?"

"No, I'm not. I got out the bag and stuffed a few things in it. And then I just sat there, on the cot, thinking about how I despised myself, and knowing that I was going nowhere."

"Good." The rocker creaked as she let it roll back again.

"What's good? That I despise myself for what happened tonight—or that I'm not going anywhere?"

"I think you can figure that out for yourself."

He dared to take a step away from the door. She had rested her head against the rocker back, shut her eyes and started rocking again. The fire was getting low. Leaving her a wide berth, he got a log from the wood basket and put it in the stove, then took the poker and stirred the coals a bit. He shut the stove door, put the poker away and sat in the easy chair.

She opened her eyes and looked across at him. For once, she spoke softly. "He's going to be fine. And he told me that you warned him not to touch the knife."

He admitted gruffly, "I should have protected him, not set the knife where he could get at it."

She laughed then. The soft sound reminded him painfully of the old days. Of the nights in his room up under the eaves at the Sierra Star, of how happy he'd been just to love her and to know that she loved him back. "Look at it this way," she said, "that's a mistake you're unlikely to make again. But don't worry, you'll mess up in a thousand other ways you never imagined you could. It's the nature of being a parent."

"If you're trying to reassure me, it's not working."

"Me? Reassure you? Hah, like that's ever gonna happen." She rose from the rocker.

He looked up at her, thinking that she was the most beautiful woman he'd ever known. And wishing she wouldn't go.

Wishing she might just sit a little longer. She wouldn't have to say—or do—anything. Just her presence would have been enough.

He would have enjoyed imagining for a few too-short minutes that they were together and staying that way.

Then again, maybe it was better if she didn't stay. After all, it was over between them. Long over. Better for him that he didn't try and pretend he could earn again what he'd thrown away by his brawling and drinking and general bad behavior.

She asked, "So can I trust you now not to run off?"

He nodded. "I'm staying right here. You might never get rid of me."

"Okay. Now I'm *really* starting to worry." She grabbed her jacket, picked up the baby monitor and went to the door, pausing to look back at him with her hand on the knob. Dimples flashed. "You made progress with him tonight. You get that, don't you?" When he only grunted, she added, "He didn't even want to come out here and say good-night to you. He did come, though, because I insisted."

"So maybe you shouldn't have insisted."

She gave him a chiding look. "Let me finish."

"Sorry."

"What I was getting at is, after he cut himself, it was *you* he wanted to drive him to the clinic."

"You're right." The realization helped. A lot. "I didn't even think about that."

"How could you? You were too busy beating yourself up."

"Yeah, I guess I was—and worrying that if I was the one driving him to see Brett, I might somehow mess that up, too."

She pulled open the door. "Good night, Bowie." And then she was gone.

The fire crackled in the stove. The workshop was cozy. Warm.

But still, it felt empty now that Glory had left.

He reminded himself—again—that she was through

with him, that what they'd had was long over and done and he needed to remember that. She was only trying to do what was right for Johnny, fighting to make sure her son didn't get hurt any more than he'd already been. Trying to give him his father so he wouldn't turn out like Bowie had—lost and angry without a dad's guiding hand.

He sat in his chair and he waited for a long time, to make sure she'd gone up to bed. Then, taking extra care to be quiet about it, he took the key she'd give him from the hook near the door and left the barn. Outside, the cold winter night seemed dipped in silver. The sky was so clear, thick with stars, and the moon just a tiny sliver hanging near the tops of the pines that covered the mountains. He stood there, midway between the house and the barn, looking up, thinking how beautiful the night was.

Finally, he shook his head and moved on, entering the darkened house on tiptoe. He used the toilet and brushed his teeth.

Back in the workshop, he banked the fire and stretched out on the narrow cot and closed his eyes—and saw Glory's face.

Not the face she showed him nowadays, but her face the way he remembered it, back in the good times. Soft, with a glow to it, eyes shining, mouth tipped up, waiting for his kiss.

For him, the face he saw alone at night was always Glory's face. In the years he'd been gone, he'd tried to banish that face from his mind and his memory. And from his heart.

Sometimes, he'd almost succeeded in making himself believe that he was over her.

Almost.

But not quite.

Chapter Seven

The next evening, Bowie took his mom out to dinner at the Nugget Steak House on Main. He joked with the owner and head waitress, Nadine Stout. And after Nadine brought their steaks and left them alone, he told his mom about the scary incident the night before.

Chastity sighed. "Poor little guy. I hate it when they bleed. But it sounds to me like it all worked out in the end."

"He wanted me to take him to the clinic so Brett could stitch him up. Me, in particular."

"That's good," said his mom. "Real good." She talked about her longtime boyfriend, Alyosha Panopopoulis, a good-natured guy who'd retired to the Flat and still worked as a handyman to bring in extra cash. She said she and Alyosha were getting along great. They liked each other—and no, she didn't think they'd get married or anything. They both enjoyed their independence.

He said, "You seem pretty happy, Ma."

"I am. I made a lot of mistakes and I regret every one of them. But I don't spend my days dwelling on them." When she said that, he thought of Glory, the night before, telling him that mistakes were part of the bargain when you were a parent. His mom added, "What matters is, I survived. And yes, you and your brothers have had your problems. But as of now, I'd say you're all doing just fine."

"Wow, Ma, did you just say you think *I'm* doing fine?"

"Yes, I did. I've been suspecting as much for a good while now. I'm glad you finally came back to town so I could tell you so to your face."

He thought about his father then, about the man he'd never known. Blake had died over a decade before. In his lifetime, he'd married any number of women—and never divorced a single one. Bowie had half siblings all over the country. Each of Blake's wives had believed she was the "only" one. But it wasn't his long string of wives that Blake was most famous—or rather *infamous*—for.

More than forty years ago, he'd kidnapped his own brother's child. A ransom in diamonds was paid, but the child, an infant at the time of the kidnapping, was never returned. When it happened, no one knew that Blake was the culprit. The whole story had finally come out around the time of Blake's death. And the kidnapped baby had been found, alive and well. And all grown up, with no idea of his real identity.

Bowie said, "Remember how sick you got, when you found out that my father was dead?"

His mom's eyes grew shadowed. "I do remember. I went to bed and didn't get up for two weeks. Worst time of my life. I finally had to face the truth then, after all those years."

He thought he knew what truth she meant. "That he was never coming back?"

She made a snorting sound. "Bowie, I might have been a fool for a very long time over a very bad man, but even I figured out a few years after you were born that we'd seen the last of him. What was harder to accept—what I refused to admit until I learned he was dead—was that I'd loved a man I didn't even know. I not only loved him, but I *kept* loving him, even though he was hardly ever home and my sons were growing up without a dad."

"Don't beat yourself up," he said, and almost smiled as the words escaped his lips. It was essentially the same advice Glory had given him the night before.

His mother shook her head. "I should have done better by you and your brothers."

"I get that. I do. Just like I should have done better by Johnny."

"You *are* doing better," she reminded him gently.

He confessed, "Johnny said he hated me that first day. I knew exactly how he felt because I'd hated my father for most of my life."

His mother asked wryly, "Do you see a pattern here?"

"Yes, I do. And it's a pattern I plan to change."

"That's the spirit." She picked up her water glass and toasted him with it.

Bowie walked her back to the B and B at around seven and went in for a last cup of coffee and a big slice of the carrot cake she'd made fresh that afternoon. He was back in the barn behind Glory's house by seven-twenty-five and got right to work on the train set for Johnny.

At seven-forty-three, Johnny tapped on the door.

Bowie grinned to himself. "It's open!"

The door swung wide. Johnny came in and shut it behind him. He was wearing a pair of Toy Story pajamas, a different jacket than the one he'd worn the night before and his boots. "I came to say 'night."

"Can you stay a few minutes?"

Johnny frowned, his small brow furrowing, as though the question required deep thought. Finally, he decided, "Well, just for a little while." He went and climbed up into the rocker where his mom had sat the night before. "I *like* rocking chairs." He rocked happily for several seconds, the old rocker creaking the whole time in a cheerful sort of way.

Bowie kept whittling.

"I got to show-and-tell about my *injury*." He said the big word with pride as, still rocking, he held up his bandaged hand. "And it hardly hurts at all today."

"I'm glad to hear that."

The rocker went silent. Johnny was watching him. "You never said who the train was for."

Bowie gave up trying to figure out just the right way to deliver the news. "It's for you."

Johnny tried not to grin, but he couldn't stop himself. "I knew it." And then he started rocking again, with enthusiasm, for maybe thirty seconds. After which he got down. "I think I better go to bed now."

Bowie wished he wouldn't go, but it seemed a little early in their new relationship to say that. So he only nodded. "Well, all right. Sleep well."

"Will you be making breakfast in the morning?"

"Yes, I will."

"Can we maybe have pancakes tomorrow, you think?"

"Yes, we can. And we will."

"I *like* pancakes." Still, he didn't make a move for the door. He twisted his mouth to the side for a moment, looking uncomfortable. And then he burst out with, "It was Bobby Winkle who said you were a drunk and a crazy man. He said that you were my *real* dad and my real dad was a drunk and a crazy man."

"I see," Bowie answered because he really wasn't sure what he should say.

"That was right after my dad died, when I was feeling really bad."

"He was a good man," Bowie said. "Your dad, I mean."

"He was the *best*. And I didn't do anything to Bobby Winkle for saying that you were drunk and crazy and that my dad wasn't my dad. But I wanted to punch him in the face. Hard." Johnny thought for a moment. "Sometimes I still want to punch him in the face."

"But you haven't."

"Nope."

Bowie set the finished train engine on the table next to his chair. "That's good. Sometimes, you have to fight. But most of the time, there are better ways to handle things. I didn't learn that the way you have. Not until I was all grown up."

"So...you think I did good?"

"I do. Yes."

"I think my dad would have said that, too."

"I think you're right."

Johnny was looking at the wooden engine. "Engines are usually black."

"Yes, they are."

"But I would like it to be blue—like Thomas, the tank engine."

"Well, all right, then. Blue it will be."

"Pancakes, huh?" Glory said the next morning when she came in the kitchen and found him whipping up the batter, the griddle nice and hot on the cooktop.

"Johnny asked for them last night."

She put the baby monitor on the counter and went and got the water going for the tea she liked. "You'll spoil him."

"That's my plan." He sent her a glance.

She was smiling—and so beautiful that it hurt him to look at her. In old jeans and a faded plaid shirt with the sleeves rolled halfway to her elbows, her brown hair loose and shining on her shoulders. She did look a little tired, though. Sera had probably kept her up half the night. She got down a mug and put a tea bag in it, poured in the hot water from the teapot he had heated for her and then gestured with the full mug at the table. "Even got the table all set, I see."

"I like to do my part."

She pulled out her usual chair and sat down. "Are you sure you're the same Bowie I used to know?"

"God, I hope not." He turned the fire down under the griddle and started pouring pancakes. The batter sizzled a little as it hit the hot surface, telling him he had the temperature right.

Johnny came bouncing in. "Pancakes. Yeah!" He went to the fridge, got out the pitcher of orange juice and carried it carefully to the table, where he poured with great concentration, his tongue caught in the side of his mouth.

Bowie flipped the pancakes. They were ready in no time. He transferred them to the platter he'd heated in the microwave.

Johnny got the first two and Glory took the two that were left. They were spreading on the butter and syrup when Sera started fussing. Glory sighed and pushed back her chair.

"Let me get her." He said it too fast and much too eagerly.

Glory almost said yes. For a moment, he could see

relief and gratitude on her sweet face. She could let him get the baby for her, and eat her pancakes before they got cold. But then she pressed her lips together. "No, it's okay. Thanks, though." Those were her words. Her eyes said something altogether different. They were guarded against him.

Upstairs in the master suite, Glory put the yowling baby to her breast. The ensuing silence was a truly lovely thing. She sat in the pretty white rocker by the window and stared out at the overcast sky. More snow was predicted for that night.

And she really did need to watch herself.

It was one thing to help Bowie and Johnny find their way to each other, one thing to establish a solid and cordial relationship with the father of her son. But it was something else altogether to let herself start playing house with him. Yeah, it was great if he wanted to help. She could use a little help around the kitchen, an extra hand at the hardware store.

But she couldn't start counting on him. She couldn't let herself be drawn in by him, let herself get too close to him.

Nights like last night, when she'd given in to her concern for him and sought him out alone...

Uh-uh. Not going to happen again. That would be plain idiocy on her part, to get involved with him now—or ever. She'd already paid and paid dearly for loving Bowie Bravo. Never again.

She just had to watch herself. Keep her distance. Remind him of the boundaries and make sure they stayed firmly in place.

From the nightstand, the picture of her and Matteo on their wedding day seemed to reproach her. She stared at her lost husband's pleasant face, his kind eyes. She still remembered that day, the day they got married, like it was yesterday. They'd exchanged their vows at the courthouse and then gone back to her mamma's house for a simple reception, just the family. Next to Johnny—and now, Sera—Matteo was the best thing that had ever happened to her. A good man, solid. Loving. Funny. Smart.

They should have had a lifetime together. She hated that he was gone. And the least she could do after losing him was to remain true to his memory and not end up throwing herself at the man who'd abandoned her and her child.

That day, the shipment of reclaimed red oak Bowie had been waiting for arrived. He got started on the table for the customer in Oregon. At lunchtime, he walked over to Main Street and ate at the diner.

On his way back to the barn, he stopped in at Rossi's Hardware Emporium, next door to the St. Thomas Bar, just to see how things were getting along there. He'd always liked the Rossi store. It was one big room, packed to the knotty-pine rafters with gardening tools and supplies, general household equipment and anything you might need for a home improvement project. One whole wall was dedicated to every nut, bolt, washer and screw of every size ever invented. As a kid, he'd loved going in that store. Matteo's dad always treated him like a regular person, not like some wild fool who might steal anything that wasn't nailed down. And Matteo took after his dad, a good man who didn't judge others. Five years ahead of Bowie in school, Matteo always greeted him with warmth and courtesy when they met on the street or in the store.

Bowie went in and saw that Glory was there at the

counter, behind the ancient National cash register. She waved when she saw him come in, but she didn't smile.

She seemed kind of preoccupied.

Or maybe it was something to do with that moment at breakfast, when he'd offered to go get Sera for her and her warm, open expression had suddenly closed tight against him. Maybe she'd decided she'd been acting too friendly with him.

Scratch the *maybe*. He knew that keep-your-distance expression when he saw it.

He went to the counter anyway. After all, as he kept reminding her, he was there to help. He saw that she had Sera, asleep in the stroller, back there with her. "Just checking in," he said. "Seeing if there's anything I can do around here...."

She pressed her lips together and shook her head. "No. Del's in the back if I need him." Del Paxton was about a hundred years old and her only employee. "I've got it handled, thanks." She smiled. But it was a flat sort of smile, all tight and strictly business.

"Anything you need from the grocery store?"

"Nope, I'm good."

He was dismissed. He got that. So he gave her a nod and he left.

At dinner that night, it was pretty much the same. She treated him with cool politeness. Johnny babbled away about his day at school. It was snowing by then. Johnny said he hoped it would "Snow and snow and never stop." He wanted to build a snowman after school the next day.

Once they'd eaten, Bowie helped clear the table. Glory put the dishes in the dishwasher and wiped down the counters without saying a word to him, avoiding eye contact the whole time.

He gave up and went out to the barn as soon as the

kitchen was in order. If she didn't want him around her, fine. He could take a hint.

Johnny came out to say good-night. He brought a book with him so that he could read Bowie a story. That was kind of fun. Johnny in the rocker and Bowie whittling in his easy chair, the fire keeping the workshop nice and toasty, Johnny reading a story about a spoon. There were lots of illustrations. Johnny would read the one or two sentences on the page and then hold up the book so Bowie could see the pictures.

It didn't take long for him to read the whole thing. "Bowie?"

"Hmm?"

"Tomorrow night, I will bring a book that a grown-up reads to a kid. And you can read it to me."

He was definitely making progress with Johnny. He told himself to be grateful for that. "Fair enough."

After Johnny left, Bowie finished the train car he was whittling and then he went outside, where the snow was still falling, soft and thick and silent, covering everything like a fluffy frozen blanket. He tipped his face up to the sky and felt the snowflakes on his cheeks, his mouth, against his eyelashes. There were maybe a couple of inches on the ground by then.

Johnny just might get lucky and be able to build himself a snowman the next afternoon.

The snow kept on until past noon the next day. And then the sun came out.

Johnny arrived home from school with one of his older cousins, one of Glory's sister Trista's kids. Glory wrapped his bandaged hand in plastic to keep the moisture out and then gave him a big snow mitten to wear on top of that. Then he and his cousin built their snowman in the front yard. Later the two of them came knocking on the work-shop door. Bowie was sanding the table he'd built. They had a lot of questions—about his tools and about why he used "old wood." He answered them as best he could.

That night, he read Johnny four chapters of *Charlie and the Chocolate Factory*. Before Johnny slogged back through the snow to the house, he got Bowie's promise that he would read the book to him every night until they reached the end.

Friday was more of the same. Glory avoided eye contact with him when he saw her in the morning at breakfast and that night at dinner. She said maybe two sentences to him all that day. He told himself he was fine with that. He was slowly forging a relationship with his son.

And that was all that mattered.

That night, he read to Johnny some more. It was great, sitting there in his easy chair, reading the story out loud. Johnny ended up pulling the rocker over closer, so he could peer over Bowie's shoulder at the illustrations. He asked a lot of questions and Bowie would stop reading so they could discuss the answers. They read a lot more than four chapters.

And it was after nine when Johnny finally put his jacket back on and returned to the house.

Saturday morning, Glory was up and waiting for him when he came in to get the breakfast started. She had her mug of tea and she was sitting at the table in a bulky brown sweater, her shoulders all hunched up. He knew just from her body language that she was pissed off about something and he was about to catch hell for whatever it was.

"I need a word with you before Johnny comes in here." She spoke low and intensely, like she was playing a spy in some espionage movie or something.

"Sure." He tried to stay upbeat.

She accused, "He came in at nine-fifteen last night."

"Sorry. We were reading and I lost track of the time."

"I want him in bed by eight. Eight-thirty at the very latest. Please send him back to the house absolutely no later than eight-fifteen. And don't make eight-fifteen a habit. Really, for all intents and purposes, his bedtime is eight o'clock." She had her mouth all pinched up again.

"If you don't watch out, Glory, your mouth might stick that way." The words were out before he remembered that he wasn't going to cop any attitudes, that he had a lot to make up for and he had no right to get all up in her face about anything.

She pinched up her mouth even tighter. "What my mouth does is no concern of yours."

He felt his temper rise. And he told it to back the hell down. "Yeah, well, no problem. I got that. Loud and clear."

She took a moment, sipped her tea, set the mug down with care. "Will you please have him back here on time at night?"

"Yeah, I'll make sure of it."

"Thanks." And she grabbed her tea, got up and left the room.

He told himself that if she wanted to be a bitch, well, that was her problem. His job right now was to fix the breakfast. He put the bacon on the griddle and assembled what he needed to make French toast.

Johnny came in still wearing his pajamas. "It's Saturday," he announced. "I *love* Saturday! Bacon. I *love* bacon. Can I help? I want to help...."

Bowie had him set the table and then allowed him to dredge the bread in the cinnamon-flavored egg mixture. Because Johnny had only one usable hand, that got a little iffy. But they worked it out.

When the food was ready, Johnny said, "I'll get Mom." He took off and returned alone. "She says she's busy and she'll eat later."

"Good enough," Bowie said, laying on the fake cheer.

After breakfast, Johnny wanted to get his sled out of the barn and use it in the big, sloping field behind the house. "Will you ride my sled with me, Bowie?"

Bowie looked down into Johnny's hopeful, happy face and he felt about ten feet tall. He felt so good that he almost didn't care that Glory was seriously pissed at him for no real reason he could understand—and had barely spoken to him for the past three days. "Yes, I'll ride your sled with you. But ask your mom first," he added. "Make sure she doesn't have something else planned." Why get her any angrier at him than she already was?

Johnny raced off to ask her.

Glory gave her permission. Bowie wrapped Johnny's stitched hand in plastic and put on the big mitten for him and they played on the hillside until around noon, when Glory called Johnny in for lunch.

She didn't invite Bowie. He tried not to be resentful that she failed to include him. After all, they more or less had an understanding that he made breakfast and was welcome at dinner, but for lunchtime, he was on his own.

He went to the diner. Charlene wasn't there. The waitress said Brand's wife usually stayed home Saturday except late in the afternoon, when she came in to close up. Bowie missed her. Charlene always took time to chat with him while he ate.

After the meal, he stopped by to see his mom. But the girl she had helping her out with the cleaning said she'd gone to Grass Valley to buy groceries.

Back at Glory's, he went inside to use the bathroom. The house was silent. Nobody home.

Feeling glum and lonely, he retreated to the workshop, where he started on the chairs that went with the table. Working helped lift his spirits, helped him to get his mind off Glory, whom he shouldn't be stewing over anyway.

That evening, he'd been invited to Charlene and Brand's. He knew Glory and the kids were going, too. But he didn't ask her if she wanted to ride over there together. He had a feeling she'd find some excuse not to ride with him—and the last thing he needed was more rejection from her.

Hadn't he had enough of that already?

He went and picked up his mom and they rode over together.

All in all, it was a good family evening, he thought. He got to hang out with his brothers and the food was great. After dinner, the older kids—Brett's two boys, Charlene's niece Mia, and Johnny—went into the living room to watch a movie.

Charlene got him aside in the kitchen when he helped her clear the table and asked him if he would consider making a crib for the baby she was having in a few months. He told her he'd be happy to, although it would be several weeks before he could have it finished.

"I'm due in mid-April," she said. "Do you think you could have it done by the first week of that month?"

"Tell you what. How about the end of February—March first at the latest?"

She beamed. "That would be great. Stay right there. I'll just get my checkbook and take care of the price right up front."

He stopped her. "Forget the checkbook. I've been trying to figure out what to get for my new niece or nephew, and now I know."

"Bowie, no." She frowned. "I can't take advantage of

you that way. Brand showed me pictures of some of the work you've done. It's just beautiful. *And* we looked you up on the Dunn Woodworkers website. I mean, you're famous. You're listed as one of the top ten woodworkers in America."

He laughed—but he was thinking about Glory again. He'd bet his best table saw that *she'd* never checked out his website. "I would say that 'famous' is a little over the top. Buck is famous." His oldest brother was a well-known author and adventurer. He lived in New York City, with his wife B.J. and their two kids.

Charlene kept after him. "I only mean, well, it just feels like I'd be taking advantage of you to ask you to build us a crib for free."

"You didn't ask, Charlene. I offered."

"But I—"

He cut her off. "It's a baby gift. Stop arguing."

She thanked him then, and let it go at last. They rejoined the others in the dining room, where the adults were having second cups of coffee after generous helpings of Charlene's excellent apple pie with homemade vanilla ice cream.

Glory's chair was empty, which didn't surprise Bowie. Sera had been fussy all evening. Glory had probably gone somewhere more private to try and feed her. He took his seat and said yes when Charlene came by with the coffeepot.

Maybe twenty minutes later, Glory appeared looking flustered, her pinned-up hair coming loose around her flushed cheeks, a still-fussing Sera in her arms. "Charlene, dinner was wonderful, but Sera's seriously colicky. I really think we're going to have to head home...."

Bowie knew he should just let it go, but he couldn't help responding to the look of misery on her face—and he hated to hear poor little Sera cry. "Here, let me have her."

Glory froze. Her mouth got that pinched look. But then Sera wailed again. And Glory gave in with a long, weary sigh. "Thanks," she said, and seemed to mean it.

He got up and took the baby. Sera kept wailing. He rubbed her little back, rocked her from side to side. "You fed her?"

Glory nodded. "And changed her...."

"Sit down," he said. "Have another cup of that awful herb tea you drink. I'll walk her around a little."

She went to the table and joined the others. He left them all in peace and took the baby on a little tour of Brand and Charlene's house—from the soaring slate entryway, up the stairs and along the upper landing that looked out over the living area below. He passed the master suite and a purple room stenciled with butterflies that he knew had to be Mia's. The third bedroom looked like a guestroom. It was simply furnished with dark blue walls. He went in there, sat on the bed and laid Sera, tummy down, along his forearm, her head cradled on his hand.

She quieted immediately. There was something about that position that seemed to soothe her.

After maybe twenty minutes, when his arm started to get tired, he tried lifting her to his shoulder again. She settled against him without a peep, sound asleep.

He considered going out to join the others again. But it was peaceful up there in the blue bedroom. And the noise and activity downstairs might just get her stirred up again. So he sat there on the bed for a while longer, listening to Sera's shallow, even breathing as she slept.

Another fifteen minutes passed. By then, he was

thinking that she was sleeping soundly enough for him to chance getting up and going downstairs.

Glory appeared in the doorway. She saw him. And she stopped there, her hand on the doorframe. For a long moment, she hesitated on the threshold, just staring at him.

And he gazed back at her. He was way too aware of how the light from the hallway brought out the gold gleams in her dark brown hair, of how big and sad her eyes looked.

She hadn't had an easy life, and he needed to remember that. First she'd gotten pregnant by the mixed-up troublemaker he used to be. And then, when she finally found a good man, he'd rolled down a mountain and ended up dead—leaving her pregnant with a second child.

It wasn't his fault that she'd lost her husband. But it *was* his fault that he'd given in to her that first night she came up to his room at the Sierra Star. It *was* his fault that he'd taken her love when he had so little to give her in return. It *was* his fault that he'd left her and Johnny, that he'd waited so long to come back and make things right.

He had a lot to make up for. He couldn't give her back the husband she'd loved. But he could quit feeling sorry for himself when she gave him a hard time, when she closed her mind against him.

It had taken *him* years to feel reasonably confident in his sobriety. How could he expect her to trust him and make nice with him when he'd barely been back in her life for two weeks?

The answer was achingly clear: he couldn't. It was going to take more than a few weeks to make it right with her.

Maybe he never could. But to have a chance of healing the deep wounds between them, he would need to be a solid, continuing presence in her life. Just as he needed to be there for Johnny. *Really* be there. Day to day.

Bowie realized that he wanted that chance. With both of them. He wanted it bad.

In his arms, Sera wiggled a little, but she didn't wake up. She yawned and nestled her head against him, nuzzling his shoulder. It came to him that he needed to be there for her, too, for Sera. And that meant it was time to start thinking about making his visit home permanent.

He made his decision at that exact moment, with Sera snuggled against his shoulder and Glory watching him from the doorway through big, haunted eyes. He was going to buy his own place in New Bethlehem Flat and open a branch of Dunn Woodworkers right there in his hometown.

Chapter Eight

Glory left the doorway and came toward him.

She held out her arms. He got up and gave her the sleeping baby.

Sera didn't even open her eyes. She made those cute little sucking motions with her tiny flower bud of a mouth and she laid her head right down on Glory's shoulder.

He whispered, "I don't know what I did to make you mad this time, Glory...."

She shook her head. Her eyes were soft by then, but still much too sad. "You've been great. Really. It's not you."

"Then what?"

"It's...hard, that's all. I don't want you to get the wrong idea about me. I don't want to get too friendly."

He got the message. Loud and clear. "You have some idea that I'm putting a move on you?"

She blinked, sucked in a sharp breath. "No. No, really. Not at all."

"Good, because I wasn't. I wouldn't. I understand that it's long over, with you and me. I get that. I'm fine with that." Well, all right, it was a lie. He wasn't fine with it in the least. But so what? She didn't need to know what he really felt. What he felt was his problem, not hers.

She repeated, so softly, "Fine with it?"

"Yeah," he lied some more. Why not? In this one case, a lie was the wisest choice. The best choice. "Just fine."

"We do need to get along...." She kissed the sleeping baby, smoothed a hand down the fine, dark curls on Sera's head. "And I'm sorry I've been such a bitch the last few days."

"It's all right."

She gave him a look from under her lashes. Humor glinted in those big eyes. "So I *have* been a bitch, then?"

He asked, still whispering, "Why do I have the feeling that no matter how I answer that one, I'm in trouble?"

"You're not in trouble," she said. "You're doing great. I appreciate all the things you do...around the house, at the store, with Johnny and Sera. You make things better for all of us. You make a difficult time a little bit easier."

A glow started in the center of him and grew until he felt the shining warmth all through him. He was a sad case, all right. A little praise from her and suddenly the world was all sunshine and rainbows.

She held out her hand. "Friends?"

He took it and studiously ignored the thrill that skittered along the surface of his skin, the kindled heat below his belt. "Friends. Yes, I would like that very much."

"I'm telling you, Angie, he hasn't got a clue."

Angie leaned closer across table of their favorite booth. "Oh, please. You should see your face every time you say his name. He *has* to see it."

"No, he doesn't. He hasn't. We're…friends now. Saturday night, at Charlene and Brand's, we came to an understanding. Since then, for the last four days, we've been getting along just great. We're on good terms now."

"Friends." Angie put a totally sarcastic spin on the word.

"You can just wipe that smirk off your face, Angela Marie. He has no intention of putting a move on me. He told me so Saturday night."

"Hah. And on top of the way that you look at him, there's also the way that *he* looks at you.…"

"It wouldn't be right."

"Why wouldn't it, exactly?"

"You know why. I'm a widow."

"Yeah, so? Widows remarry. They do that a lot."

"Marriage?" Glory gaped. "Who said a word about marriage?"

"Okay, forget marriage for now."

"Forget marriage, period. What are you talking about? I'm not marrying Bowie. And this isn't seven years ago. He no longer has any interest in marrying me."

"You keep saying that, as if you're going to convince yourself. You've always loved him and he's always loved you."

"I loved my husband."

"I know you did."

"You just said…"

"Glory, you loved Matteo and you were a good wife to him. That doesn't mean you don't love Bowie, too—but in a different way, a way that scares you, a way that broke your heart once. Now, well, Bowie's a changed man. He's a good man, and he's made a go of his life after just about everyone was sure there was no hope for him. Everybody sees that. Everybody but you. If you gave him a chance now, things would be different."

"Uh-uh, you're so wrong."

"You seriously don't see how much Bowie has changed?"

"I see it, yes. And I'm happy for him—happy for my son, too. Johnny needs his father. But you can stop talking about second chances. What Bowie and I had, that's all in the past."

Angie didn't say anything. She sipped her iced tea and let her disbelieving expression do the talking for her.

Glory sent a quick glance around the diner. They'd met for lunch later than usual that day and the place was pretty much cleared out, which was good. There was no one nearby to hear a word they said. Still, she leaned close to her sister again and pitched her voice too low for anyone else to have the slightest chance of hearing. "Matteo's been gone only six and a half months."

"I know. It's sad that you lost him. That Johnny lost him. That Sera will never know him. But the point is, he's gone. He's not coming back. Wearing sackcloth and ashes your whole life isn't going to prove a thing to anyone. Except that maybe you and Aunt Stella have more in common than you like to admit."

Glory gasped. "I do not believe you just said that. I am nothing like Aunt Stella."

"Well, Glory, who'll tell you the truth, if not me? You are acting a little like Aunt Stella, seriously. All self-righteous and gloomy."

Glory drew her shoulders back. "I am not self-righteous."

"Before you know it, you'll start carrying a rosary around with you, praying to the holy virgin under your breath everywhere you go."

"Why, you..." Glory reached across the table and smacked her sister on the hand.

"Ouch!" Angie cried. And then she started laughing.

Angie's laughter was contagious. Glory started laughing, too. They collapsed in a fit of giggles, right there in the booth.

Eventually, when they got control of themselves again, Glory leaned close and said very low, "I don't know why we're talking about this. Even if Bowie was maybe still interested—which he is not—I just had a *baby,* for cryin' out loud. I can't be doing anything like that for weeks yet. And you know what? I'm *glad* I can't. I'm glad Bowie and I can just try and get along, just maybe learn how to be friends and not get into any of that stuff that got us in trouble in the first place."

Angie made a knowing sound. "Those weeks you are talking about will be gone before you know it. They're almost half over now."

"They are not."

"Yeah. Think about it. It was two weeks on Monday since Sera was born. And today is already Wednesday."

Glory did not want to think about it. "I know what day it is. Sheesh, rub it in, will you?"

"I'm only saying time flies, you know? And when the usual six weeks are over, *then* what will you do?"

"Oh, come on, I'm not some barnyard animal. I'll exercise a little self-control."

"Hah."

"And anyway, by then, Bowie will probably be gone back to Santa Cruz."

"I wouldn't count on that...."

Glory looked at Angie sharply. "What are you saying? Things are going well with him and Johnny. He's not staying here forever."

Angie blinked and glanced away.

Glory got a sinking feeling. "Okay, what do you know? You'd better tell me."

In the stroller beside the booth, Sera let out a squeak and then a tiny gurgle.

Angie asked, "You want me to take her?"

"Don't change the subject. What do you know?"

"Oh, crap. Brett is going to be so pissed at me. He told me not to say anything. He told me to stay out of it, that it was Bowie's place to tell you."

"Angie, tell me what?"

Angie let her shoulders sag and blew out a guilty breath. "Yesterday, when Bowie and Brett and Brand went to lunch at the Nugget together?"

"Yeah? What?"

"Bowie asked them to keep an eye out for a place here in town, a couple of acres with a house on it and room to build a workshop and an office for a new branch of his carpentry business."

Stunned and more than a little angry, Glory whispered, "He's moving back to town permanently?"

"Yep, that's about the size of it."

It's his choice if he wants to live here in town again, Glory said to herself several times that day.

Also, the more she thought it over, the better it sounded. It would be better for Johnny if Bowie returned to the Flat to stay. And better for her, too, because she wouldn't have to send her son away for him to spend time with his father. Better for Chastity, who seemed so happy to have her youngest son nearby again.

It was better in just about *every* way.

Except one.

If he stayed, temptation stayed with him.

Because he did tempt her. Without even trying to. He behaved in a completely respectful way with her. He never said anything that might lead her to believe that he remembered what they'd once shared. He never sent her a single intimate or smoldering look.

And still, every day, every hour, every minute she was near him the old, sweet memories came back all the more clearly.

The way she had chased him.

Oh, yes, she had. Just shamelessly chased him. Back then, he'd seemed determined not to take her up on what she was offering him. She used to find reasons to walk in front of him, just get her hips to swaying, to try and give him some kind of an idea of what she was offering.

And she never wasted a single chance to get him talking. She'd asked him the silliest questions. Did he prefer white bread or wheat? (Wheat.) Which of his mother's famous muffin recipes was his favorite? (Pumpkin.) Did he like the Cranberries? (The *what?*) She'd ended up explaining to him that the Cranberries were her favorite group. She even burned him a CD of their best songs. He'd said he really liked them and he played the CD she'd made for him over and over again until she teased him that he would wear it out.

And why in heaven's name was she thinking about all that?

Now, lately, with him around constantly, in and out of her house, the past seemed so much closer, so much more real to her. It felt almost as though it had all happened yesterday.

The last week or so, at night when she would lie in bed in the dark, with Sera quiet at last—the time she should have been sleeping—she would recall acutely the feel of his mouth over hers. A perfect fit. And the scent of him, like the pines and the wind in the springtime, all green and fresh with new life.

She would feel all over again the sense of hope and promise she'd known back then, to be in love with Bowie Bravo and have a whole life of loving him ahead of her. She'd had no idea then that her love wouldn't be enough for him, that he had some big-time demons and those demons would win out over her love every single time. She'd been too young and foolish to see that when she needed him to be strong for her, he would be drunk and disorderly and unable to hold a job.

Yes, he was different now. Better. Calmer. So much stronger. Apparently, her fears about the money he'd been sending for Johnny were unfounded. Those big checks were not ill-gotten gains after all. He'd made a success of his carpentry work.

Glory was glad for him, glad for Johnny, too.

But for the two of them as a couple, it was too late. They'd had their chance and blown it.

Yes, she still wanted him. A lot.

But desire wasn't enough. Not when the love was gone.

"You okay, Glory?" Bowie asked her during dinner.

She faked a bright smile. "I'm fine."

"You seem kind of…I don't know. Like there's something weighing on your mind."

It made a tender spot within her, that he noticed. That he cared enough to ask her if something was wrong. But she knew that she needed to just blow it off, let it go. The whole point, after all, was not to get too close to him, not to go confiding her feelings to him, which would only open the door on all the things she kept telling herself were *not* going to happen between them.

So she shrugged and ate another bite of Swiss steak and gave no reply. He left it at that.

But later, after Johnny returned from his nightly visit to the workshop, after she tucked him in bed and checked on Sera, when she went downstairs for a last cup of tea in her quiet kitchen, she heard the back door open. She sat so still, her hands wrapped around the comforting warmth of her favorite mug, her heart bouncing wildly under her breastbone.

His careful footsteps approached, coming toward her along the short hall that led past the laundry room and the downstairs bath. And then he was there. He paused in the doorway and then came forward, into the kitchen with her. She watched him come closer. He wore the same flannel shirt and faded jeans he'd been wearing earlier. She thought that he was probably the best-looking man she'd ever known, with those blue, blue eyes and that knife blade of a nose that was only a little bit crooked from being broken more than once. There was also that fine cleft in his chin that all the Bravo boys had. The broad shoulders, lean hips and powerful arms didn't hurt any, either.

He pulled out the chair across from her and sat. "Got a minute?"

She raised her mug, took a slow sip. "Sure." Her voice betrayed none of her inner turmoil. At least she could be grateful for that.

"Johnny's hand seems pretty well healed."

Brett had taken the stitches out the day before—and was that why he'd sought her out tonight? To talk about Johnny's hand? "Yeah. Kids tend to heal up pretty quick."

Bowie shifted in the chair, leaning back, sticking a hand in his pocket. He pulled something out, laid it on the table between them.

She smiled when she saw what it was. "Your old Swiss Army knife." The red handle was worn from years of use, the white-cross logo rubbed away to not much more than a pale shadow against the red.

"My uncle Clovis gave it to me..."

"For Christmas, the year you were seven," she finished for him around the sudden thickness in her throat.

His eyes held hers. "You remember." She said nothing. It seemed wiser not to speak. Clovis was Chastity's brother. He was also Brand's mostly retired partner in Cook and Bravo, Attorneys at Law. Their office was across from the courthouse, on the same street as the clinic. "Uncle Clovis never taught me how to use it, though." He turned his hands over, stared at his long, scarred fingers, his calloused palms. "Cut the hell out of myself more than once, learning how. I always wished I had a dad, you know? A real dad who lived with us and taught me things like how to use a pocketknife."

She got his drift then. "You want to give that knife to Johnny."

"I do." Suddenly, he was so very formal-sounding. "And to teach him how to use it. With your permission."

"He's only six."

"Seven in May."

She couldn't help it. She chuckled. "You sound like him. 'I'm six and a *half*, Mom.'" She imitated Johnny's insistent tone.

"Well, he is. And I notice he does fine with a steak knife. Plus, I don't think it's a good idea to protect kids from everything that might possibly hurt them. A kid needs a chance to work with tools, to learn to master them."

It just so happened she agreed with him. "You'll teach

him to use it *and* drive him to the clinic the next time he cuts himself bad enough to need stitches?"

A slow smile curved the mouth that had once fit against hers so perfectly. "My plan is for there not to be a next time."

"Bowie, you're a parent now. You need to get used to the concept that there is always a next time. Sometimes I think kids were put on this earth to mess with each and every one of our well-thought-out plans."

"Okay. I get it."

"You get what?"

"Yeah, I'll take him to the clinic *if* he needs stitches again."

"All right, then. We have a deal."

"And I want to teach him to whittle, too—not with a pocketknife. For whittling, he'll use a fixed blade."

"Oh, I can't wait."

"A little heavy on the irony, aren't you, Glory?"

"Just take your time about it, please. Teach him right."

"I will, I promise you. I'm also thinking he should have a dog."

She slanted him a look—and hit him with what she knew. "Good thing you've decided to move back to town. He can have a dog at *your* place."

He scratched his sculpted cheek. "Angie?"

"This is how it works. You tell your brother, he tells his wife, and there's a very good chance that my sister is going to tell me."

He folded his hands on the tabletop and stared at them for a moment or two. "I guess I should have figured that."

"Guess you should have."

"I did plan to tell you."

"When?"

"Tonight, right now—given that I managed to work up the nerve."

She looked into her mug and thought about getting up and brewing a second cup. But in the end, she pushed the mug away and stayed in her seat.

He spoke again, softly. "I was kind of scared that you would be mad about my moving back here."

She tipped her head to the side and studied his face. He looked hopeful, she thought. That maybe this time she wouldn't jump all over him? Probably. "I was a little angry at first. But then I thought it over. It's best for Johnny if you move back to town."

"I was thinking the same thing." He pushed back his chair.

She knew he was leaving and she hated how much she wished that he wouldn't. But then he only went to the counter, got down a glass, filled it with water from the tap and came back to settle into the chair across from her again.

He drank half the water, set it down on the tabletop, turned the glass in a slow circle. "I was surprised when I heard that *you'd* come back to town."

"You mean five years ago?"

"Yeah. First I got the news that you'd taken Johnny and moved to New York City to work for B.J. as a nanny." B.J. was his brother Buck's wife. "I heard you were taking online classes, too, to get a college degree."

"Who did you hear all that from?"

"Ma sent me letters. And my brothers wrote to me, too."

"You never sent *me* an address where I could write to you." She knew she sounded accusing again. So what? She *felt* accusing.

"I didn't send Ma or my brothers an address, either.

At first I didn't have one to send. But then they sent my half brother Tanner out to find me. He's a private investigator. Lives in Sacramento?"

She nodded. "I think Brand has mentioned him once or twice."

"His mother was Lia. She had Tanner and two daughters by Blake." Bowie smiled but there was little humor in it. "He was a busy guy, dear old Dad." He kept turning that half-full glass. "So Tanner found me and told me he was telling Ma and my brothers where to get in touch with me. By then, I was thinking I should have told them myself. So I was glad to get their letters. And grateful to hear about you and Johnny, to know that you were getting along all right, managing better without me than you ever did with me around to mess things up for you. Ma asked in one of her letters if she could give you my address. I wrote back and asked if you'd asked for it. She said that you'd told her you didn't want to hear anything about me. Ma said you told her that if I wanted to contact you, I knew where to find you."

"That's right. It's what I told her." She would have given anything—a kidney, every last ounce of her pride—to have gotten one letter from him back then. But now, slowly, she was coming to understand what a mess he'd been in those days, that it hadn't been a simple matter of him snapping out of it and behaving like a normal person. During that time, he really hadn't been capable of the simple actions that mean so much.

He asked again. "So why did you come back from New York?"

She shrugged. "I got homesick, that's all. I'm from the Flat. It's a lot of who I am. My family drives me up the wall, but I missed them so much. And I missed your mamma, too. Finally, I couldn't stand it anymore. I just had to come home."

"You ever get that college degree?"

"What? Nobody told you?"

"They didn't tell me *everything*. And I never had the nerve to ask them. I kind of figured it was one thing if they volunteered stuff about you and Johnny. But as soon as I asked them…" His voice trailed off.

Her throat clutched tight again. "What? Say it."

He didn't answer right away. She became certain he wouldn't. But then, he surprised her. "I didn't feel I had any right, okay? No right to ask about you when I wasn't…there for you. Or for Johnny."

A loose curl of hair kept tickling her cheek. She smoothed it away. "Okay, I guess I get that."

He braced his elbows on the table, so his strong forearms surrounded both the water glass and the old pocketknife. He leaned in across them, closer to her. "So did you get your degree?"

"Yes, I did. I have a B.A. in business." She still got a feeling of satisfaction just saying it. "Took six years, but I did it. I graduated last June. And then, a month later, Matteo died."

He scanned her face. "That must have been brutal."

"Brutal," she echoed. "Yeah, that's a good word for it." She looked down into her empty mug. "He was so proud of me. It was…such a happy time. I earned my degree. We had found out I was pregnant.…" Her voice was barely a whisper. "And then he died." She glanced up again. Bowie's eyes were waiting. She opened her mouth and told him more. "I went to work for him at the hardware store when I got back in town from New York. Matteo was good to me. Patient. Kind. He paid more than minimum wage and gave me health insurance. I was so grateful. And he understood, about my being a single mom. When Johnny got sick, Matteo didn't get all on my case because I needed a day off. And the first time he asked me out, he was so nervous, just falling all over himself, stammering a little, wondering if maybe I might possibly want to join him for a steak at the Nugget...." She closed her eyes, let out a low groan. "Oh, what am I doing? Telling you all this. You don't need to hear this...."

"Glory, come on, look at me."

She made herself do it, made herself open her eyes and face him. He gazed back at her, so calm and unruffled, eyes like the ocean on a clear, windless day. So unlike the Bowie she used to know. Unlike...and yet, still the same, deep down somewhere. At the core.

He said, "What you're saying is nothing I hadn't already pretty much figured out."

"Maybe so, but that doesn't make it any less...oh, I don't know. Inappropriate, I guess."

"It's just the truth, right?"

"Yeah, but still. Can we talk about something else?"

That slow, irresistible smile again. "Sure."

"Those first checks you sent me?"

"I hope they helped."

She confessed, "I really needed them. I cashed them, spent them on shoes and groceries, on the essentials."

"Good, that's why I sent them. I didn't have what it took, to come myself, to write you a damn letter now and then. But at least after I started working for Wily, I had a little cash I could contribute."

"I want to tell you..." She hardly knew how to go on.

"Please, I'm listening."

"Bowie, I...as the checks got larger, I was sure you must have done something illegal to get that money."

He shrugged. "Yeah, well, I wasn't communicating, was I?"

"No, you weren't."

"You were in the dark. I guess I'm not surprised you assumed the worst. And I don't blame you."

She put her hands over her mouth, let out a pained laugh and then dropped them, palms flat, on the table. "Well, *I* blamed *you*."

"I kind of gathered that."

She didn't know why she wanted him to hear all this. She only knew that it was something she suddenly just *had* to tell him. "After Matteo and I got married, I opened a special savings account. I put every check you sent from then on into it." She glanced toward the dark window that faced the backyard. "I was afraid to spend it, in case someone showed up to take it back."

"Well, great." He sounded sincere. "That means Johnny's got a head start on his college education."

"I can't believe you're not offended."

He blew out a breath. "I am, a little. But I'm thinking that's my problem, not yours."

She looked at him, amazed all over again at the changes in him. "You're so…even-tempered now. You always used to be on a hair trigger, always angry. And you always used to boss me around."

"Well, I tried to. You never were real big on letting anyone tell you what to do—and the truth is, I felt so far beneath you. And I was always afraid that I would lose you. And guess what? I got exactly what I was so scared of. I pushed you away. And I lost you."

"I just, well, I never…"

"Never, what?"

"Never in my life did I even dream that we might end

up sitting at my kitchen table like we are right now, telling each other these things."

"It was always too damn hard to talk to me," he said softly. "Wasn't it?"

"Yeah. I finally realized it was never going to work with us. I accepted that."

"I know." It was a simple statement of fact.

"And I have to tell you…"

"Yeah?"

"At first, when you came back, I was just waiting for you to mess up again."

"Yeah, well, I expected that."

"And then, because you haven't messed up, I sometimes find myself wondering what you've done with the real Bowie."

"I *am* the real Bowie."

She made a show of squinting at him, hard. "You sure?"

He made a low sound, a short, rough laugh. "I still feel a lot of the same bullheaded unreasonable crap I always felt. I just learned that I don't have to act on every little emotion that gets my heart beating faster. Wily Dunn taught me that. Wily would say, *'Just 'cause you got feelings, son, that don't mean you* have *to exercise 'em.'*"

"He sounds like a wise man."

"He was. I miss him. So much."

She dared to suggest, "He sounds like a good father, like the father you never had."

"Yes, he was. And I'm grateful to have known him, to have had him in my life, even if he was gone way too soon." Bowie picked up the water glass and pushed back his chair. "I'm also glad that we had this talk."

"So am I." And she was. Maybe too glad.

He took his glass to the sink, crossing behind her to

get there. She kept her gaze straight ahead, didn't allow herself to turn and watch him. He was leaving, going back across the yard to his half of the barn. She reminded herself that it was past time for him to go.

"Don't forget your Swiss Army knife." She picked it up from the table and stood.

He came back in three long strides and he was right there, beside her. She stared up at him, feeling dazed and a little disoriented, like a woman suddenly roused from a deep sleep. All the breath seemed to have fled her body.

She made herself draw in air. And that only brought the scent of him into her. Spring wind. Wood shavings and evergreen. So tempting. So well-remembered.

"Thanks." He took the knife from her hand, his rough fingers cradling hers for a sweet, endless moment, sending hot flares of sensation zipping up and down her arm.

She wanted him to let go, step back, give her room to gather her defenses, to regain her certainty that nothing intimate or crazy was ever going to happen between them again.

And at the same time, she knew she yearned for exactly the opposite: for him to move even closer, for him to put his strong arms around her. For the feel of his perfect mouth again. At last. Touching hers.

After all these years.

He whispered, "Glory?" using her name to frame the impossible question.

That was her final signal. This was the crucial last moment. Her response was the key.

A simple no. The slightest shake of her head. It wouldn't have taken much. She knew him better now than she had the day he came to her out of the storm. She knew the strong, determined man he had become.

Such a man didn't need much urging to do the right thing.

She should give him that urging. She was all too achingly aware of that, of what she *should* do.

And still, she held off. She let the last moment draw out forever.

She gazed up at him, transfixed, while somewhere in the wiser part of her mind, she frantically checked off the reasons why she needed to call a halt right now. She had loved him beyond reason and he had broken all his promises. He had deserted her. And there had been Matteo who was so good to her. Good *for* her...

But Angie was right. Matteo was gone.

And Glory was still very much alive.

And lately, in the darkest part of the night, when she reached out her hand and touched only the cool, empty sheets on the other side of the bed, it wasn't Matteo she was reaching for.

"Bowie," she whispered. It was her answer. It was her *yes*.

He recognized it as such. He framed her face in his two rough, warm hands. He said her name again. "Glory..." He said it raggedly that second time, as though he was pulling it up from the deepest part of himself.

And he lowered his mouth to cover hers.

Chapter Nine

It was the wrong thing, to kiss her.

Bowie knew it.

He kissed her, anyway.

Because her eyes told him yes when she whispered his name.

Because she was everything he'd ever wanted, everything that mattered, everything he'd thrown away in his sad, desperate spiral down to his own personal rock-bottom. She was all that he'd known he had no right to ever hold again.

He found her as he remembered, apples and rain and unimaginable sweetness.

Just as he remembered…

Only better.

It was the wrong thing, to kiss her. And yet how could it be wrong when it felt so exactly, perfectly, essentially right?

She lifted her small, soft body toward him and he felt

her breasts against his chest, fuller than they once were. So tempting. Already, he was growing hard.

Her cool, tender hands came up. She laid her palms against his chest and then slid them up, until her fingers linked around his neck. Her mouth opened beneath his on a long, sweet sigh.

It was too much. It was everything. Glory. In his arms again at last.

He gathered her closer, deepened the kiss, easing his tongue in where it was so warm and wet. She moaned a little. He drank in the sound.

But it had to end. It couldn't go anywhere.

He understood that. His blood pounded in his veins and his body ached to be with her, the way it used to be, all those years ago.

Used to be...

And never would again.

When she brought her hands back down between them and laid them against his chest once more, she hardly exerted any pressure at all. He could have easily overridden her, could have pretended she wasn't asking him to stop.

But he didn't override her. He was long past that kind of pretending.

It tore his heart in half to do it, but he lifted his mouth from hers.

Those big eyes regarded him, so soft. Brandy-brown. "Good night, Bowie."

"Good night." He let her go.

"When?" Angie demanded. "When did this happen?"

Glory ate a potato chip, slowly. "Last Wednesday night."

"Bowie kissed you—he actually *kissed* you?"

"That's what I said."

"A *week* ago? And you never even *called* me?" Angie asked the two questions at full volume.

It was safe for them to speak above a whisper today. They were sharing lunch at Angie's house, down by the river. Brett was at the clinic and the kids were in school. Sera was sleeping in a nest of pillows in the living room.

Glory picked up a triangle of chicken-salad sandwich and started to take a bite. But she couldn't. Her sister's eyes reproached her. She set the sandwich down. "Look, I shouldn't have let it happen. And it's not going to happen again." Angie only stared at her. "You can just stop looking at me like that, please. It was just…one of those moments, you know?"

"One of what moments, exactly?"

"We were talking…."

"You and Bowie, you mean?"

Glory nodded. "*Really* talking. About the past, you know? About his moving to town and about Johnny. And then, Bowie got up to go and…oh, I don't know. It just happened."

"Let me get this straight. You kissed Bowie for the first time in…what, seven years?"

"Actually, it was seven years and three months ago. In October. October 28, to be specific. It was the day before he went behind my back and told my parents I was pregnant to get them to put the pressure on me to marry him. I refused to kiss him ever again after that. I mean, until last Wednesday."

Angie gave her one of those way-too-knowing looks. "October 28. Amazing. You still remember the exact date."

Glory put up a hand. "Don't say it, please."

Angie put on her innocent look. "Say what, Glory?"

Glory picked up her sandwich again, resolutely bit into

it and chewed. Thoroughly. "It's been a week since it happened, okay? And there has been nothing—nothing—since then. I see him two, three, even four times a day. I have breakfast and dinner with him. Nothing."

"Nothing," Angie echoed, but in such a way that she implied *everything.*

"Nothing." Glory said it again because she knew that Angie was not getting the point. "It was…a fluke, that's all. Just one of those things."

"Was it good?"

"What do you mean was it good?"

"You know exactly what I mean."

Glory ate another potato chip. And another after that. Angie watched her, a relentless kind of watching. Finally, Glory cried, "Yes! All right? It was good. It was *really* good. And I want to kiss him again. I want to do a whole lot more than kiss him. I seriously do." She stuffed yet another chip in her mouth and chewed it furiously. "I don't know what it is about that man. He's my weakness. He's always been my weakness. All these years, everything that's happened, and still the feeling is there. I mean, come on, that can't be normal, can it? Everybody knows that the whole sex thing lasts only for so long between two people."

Angie was smiling much too sweetly. "So they say."

Glory groaned. "I'm happy for you and Brett. I mean, it's great if you two can keep the passion going."

"Yes, it certainly is."

"But I would just as soon *not* have that going on with me and Bowie."

"Well, maybe the feeling will go away. It could happen."

"Hah. That's not what you think, Angie. I can see on your face what you really think."

"I'm only trying to be supportive."

"Hmm. He's teaching Johnny to whittle, did I tell you that?"

"Johnny hasn't been back to the clinic for more stitches, so I'm guessing that's working out all right."

"Johnny loves it. He's always in the workshop lately. As soon as he gets home from school, he rushes right through his homework so he can get out there and be with Bowie—who is whittling him a train set. Did I tell you that?"

"Yeah, you did."

"Ah, that's right. I guess I did." Glory stared out the window near the table. The sky was gunmetal gray and a blanket of snow covered the ground. Sometimes lately, it seemed that it had been winter forever, that the spring would never come.

Angie asked, gently, "Is Johnny calling him dad yet?"

"Not yet. It will be a while, I think. But I can feel it coming."

That night, after Johnny went back across the yard to the house, Bowie watched for a light in the kitchen window. The light would mean Glory had come downstairs for a last mug of tea.

She came down most nights. He would see the light in the window and make himself wait to go inside and brush his teeth until at least ten minutes after the light went out. He'd been doing that—making himself wait to go inside at night until she was settled upstairs—the whole time he'd been staying in the workshop.

The past week, though, he'd wanted to go in while she was still up, to talk to her, just the two of them, with honesty and frankness, the way they'd finally done last Wednesday night.

The night he'd kissed her.

The night she'd kissed him back.

The kiss had been amazing. Too bad it had also ruined everything. He knew she regretted it. He'd seen regret in her eyes every day since then, at breakfast and again at dinner—and any other time of the day he happened to be in the same room with her. He'd seen her regret and her worry that he was going to try and kiss her again.

Well, he wasn't. No way. Even though the memory of that kiss would probably dog him to his grave—the memory of that kiss, and all the kisses they'd shared way back then.

He loved kissing her. He loved the feel of her small, soft body against him, the taste of her mouth, the scent of apples and rain....

Too bad. Memories would be all he would have from now on and he accepted that.

He'd also decided that he couldn't sit out here every night and wait for her to go to bed, all the while wanting only to be in there with her. It was silly.

Stupid.

Why shouldn't he go in and visit with her? They were two adults who had shared a kiss when they probably shouldn't have. It wasn't the end of the world.

He had things to tell her. He needed to talk with her. *They* needed to get over it and move on.

That night, the minute the kitchen light popped on, he left the workshop and headed for the house. No hesitation. He wasn't giving himself a chance to reconsider. He mounted the back-porch steps with determination and made no effort to be quiet about opening the back door, shutting it behind him and marching down the short hall to the kitchen.

She stood at the peninsula of counter next to the cooktop wearing jeans and a soft-looking sweater the reddish-brown color of cinnamon, fixing her tea. When he entered the kitchen, she whirled to face him. Her eyes went wide and worried.

"Bowie!" She actually put her hand against her throat the way women did in the movies when they were afraid the bad guy was going to jump their bones. "What's happened? What's wrong?"

Just say it. Just spit it out. "Glory, look, I'm sorry. I shouldn't have kissed you. I was way out of line. It won't happen again, okay?"

She gulped. She actually gulped. And she still had her hand at her throat. "Uh. Yeah. Sure." She sucked in a quivery breath. "Okay…"

"I mean that. I swear that."

"And I…I hear you. I do." Slowly, she lowered her hand to her side. Was that a good sign? How the hell would he know?

Keep talkin', buddy. "Because I really do want us to get along. To be friends, like we agreed that night at Charlene and Brand's house. I want us to be able to, you know, talk to each other like two grown-up people who have to raise their kid together, even if they *aren't* together, even if they…" Crap. What was he babbling about? He was ridiculous. He didn't need to *keep* talking; he needed to shut the heck up. "Crap." He said it out loud, as if that was going to help the situation any. And then, before she could ask him to please just leave, he marched past the kitchen area to the breakfast nook where he yanked out a chair, dropped into it, braced his elbows on the table and put his head in his hands. "What am I talking about?" he asked no one in particular. "I have no idea what I'm saying…."

A silence ensued. A really long, painful one. He refused to look up and see the disgusted expression on her face.

Finally, he heard her footsteps. She pulled out the chair across from him and sat in it. He heard her put down her mug of tea on the table. "Bowie." Did he hear a hint of laughter in her voice?

"Oh, great," he muttered. "Now you're laughing at me—not that I blame you. I am pretty damn laughable."

"I am not laughing at you. And come on, you can't sit there with your head in your hands all night."

"Watch me."

"Come on…"

He let his hands drop to the table. "What?" he demanded.

Glory met his eyes and told herself she did not feel bad because he was sorry that he'd kissed her. No, not at all. It was better that he regretted it. She was more than happy to hear that he wasn't going to try and kiss her again.

"You're right," she said. "We should get past this."

His scowl fell away. "You mean that?"

She wrapped her hands around her mug of tea and took comfort from the warmth. "What you said is true. We have Johnny to think about and we need to get along."

"Whew. That is so good to hear."

She picked up the mug, took a careful sip. "Let's put it behind us."

"Agreed," he said.

"Good," she said.

"It's…the best thing."

"You're right. It is.…"

Another silence. The really awkward kind. Finally, he spoke again. "Did you hear that I made an offer on the Halstotter place?"

"No. When?"

"Yesterday." He lifted one sculpted shoulder in a half shrug. "I wanted to be the first to tell you, but around this town, word gets out fast."

"I hadn't heard."

"Well, now you have."

She said, "That's a nice property—a beautiful house, and that great big hangar of a shed. Lots of level ground and easy to get to." She'd been inside that house once, for a dinner party, when Matteo was still alive. It had a gorgeous modern kitchen, both a living room and a family room and five large, bright bedrooms. "Did they take your offer?"

He chuckled. "Are you kidding? In this market? They jumped on it. I heard back from Tillie Manus this morning." Tillie was a local Realtor. Almost everyone in town used her when they bought or sold property. "My offer has been accepted." He looked so pleased about it.

"Wow," she said, injecting a lot more enthusiasm than she felt into the word. Lord. She was going to miss him when he went. And not only because she'd come to count on him and all the help he gave her around the house. Oh, what was her problem, anyway? It was good, she reminded herself, that he would soon be moving to his own place. He couldn't stay out there in her barn forever. The guy had a right to get on with his life. "When will you take possession?"

"Five weeks. The second week of March. The house is fine, move-in ready."

A month, and he wouldn't be in and out of her house anymore. He'd be at his own place. Johnny would visit him there, stay with him there....

"Congratulations," she said and tried really hard to mean it.

She must have succeeded. He gave her that slow smile, the one that turned her silly heart to mush. "Thanks, Glory. I'm excited. I…" His sentence died, barely begun as the fussy little whines started from the monitor on the counter by the sink.

They sat there, neither moving, just looking at each other, as Sera progressed beyond the fussy stage and let out a wail. Bowie winced. He hated it when she cried.

She teased, "Aren't you going to volunteer to go and get her?"

He looked at her steadily. "You know I want to. I figure you'll tell me if you want me to do it."

She waved a hand. "Go on. Go."

He was out of that chair and headed for the stairs in an instant. She watched him go, and for the first time she felt grateful. Truly grateful. That he'd come back to town at last, that he was working things out with Johnny.

That he adored her daughter and her daughter seemed to feel the same way about him.

Somehow, Bowie Bravo had become a very good man.

And good men, as every woman knows, are much too hard to find.

"Well," Angie said in a disgusted tone a week later, "it's obvious he's interested, or he *would* be interested, if you gave him so much as a hint that you *wanted* him to be interested."

Glory settled the baby a little more comfortably against her breast. They were at Glory's house that day. She'd made vegetable soup and grilled-cheese sandwiches. "How would you know if he would or could be interested?"

"What do you mean how would I know? Haven't we

been through this already? I've seen you together. The attraction is…palpable."

"Palpable." Glory scowled. "That's a very big word for something that's none of your business."

Angie let out a laugh. "If it's none of my business, then you should stop talking to me about it." She took a bite of her sandwich. "Mmm. Soooo good. You always did make the best grilled cheese. I think it's that panini pan you use. Makes them crispy on the outside, and melts the cheese to a truly decadent gooeyness."

"Are you changing the subject?"

"You mean the one that's none of my business?"

"He's moving out in four weeks."

"So? He'll still be in town. That way, when you finally stop lying to yourself and make your move, you won't have to drive all the way to Santa Cruz to seduce him."

Glory let her mouth drop open. "I do not believe you just said that to me."

"Good point. Denial is always an option." Angie pushed back her chair. "More iced tea?"

The days went by much too fast. Bowie went to Santa Cruz for two days on business. When he returned, Johnny ran out to meet him. Bowie grabbed him up and twirled him around. Glory watched them from the bay window in the family room and couldn't help smiling at the sight.

Bowie finished the train set for Johnny, even painted every car to Johnny's exact specifications. Johnny had the set in his room now, along with a giant tub of blocks of all sizes and shapes that Bowie had made from scraps of lumber.

The whittling lessons seemed to be progressing, too. Johnny had whittled a rather crooked-looking squirrel and a small, round creature he said was a guinea pig. Now he was working on a raccoon.

Nearly every evening when Glory went downstairs for that final cup of tea, Bowie came inside to sit with her. They talked. About nothing. About everything.

Another week flew past. And suddenly, it was the last Monday in February and time to go to the clinic for her six-week checkup.

Angie, who'd gotten her master's degree in nursing a couple of years before and become a nurse practitioner, did the exam and gave Glory a clean bill of health. She also wrote a scrip for a birth-control pill that was progestin-only and safe for nursing mothers. "Never hurts to be prepared," she said with a pleasant, professional smile as she ripped the prescription off the pad.

Glory accepted the scrip even though she did not approve of herself for doing so. And then, before Johnny got home from school, she drove down to Grass Valley and filled it.

The instructions for the pills said she would be fully protected within forty-eight hours of taking the first one. She put the pill case away in her underwear drawer and told herself that Angie was right. It was good to be prepared.

Not that she *needed* to be prepared.

In the morning, when she got up, she took the pill case from her drawer, popped the first pill out of its protective plastic bubble and swallowed it. As soon as she did that, she wished that she hadn't. She did not, after all, actually plan to seduce the father of her son.

"Denial is always an option." Her sister's knowing voice echoed in her brain.

Was she in denial?

It was a definite possibility.

But if she *did* try and seduce him, in forty-eight hours, given that she took the second pill, she would be protected from getting pregnant again, at least. The other consequences of such a foolish action would still be hers to confront, the *emotional* consequences. The ones she really ought to be considering more thoroughly.

Glory put the case away and went down to breakfast, where Bowie stood at the cooktop stirring a pan of oatmeal. Her heart gave a lurch in her chest and her pulse beat faster, just at the sight of him standing there in her kitchen. His hair was a little longer than it had been when he first showed up at her door. And his eyes were like oceans she could happily drown in.

He smiled at her. "Morning."

"Morning." She got down her mug and brewed her tea and tried not to think that Johnny had a sleepover birthday party at his cousin's on Friday. Well beyond the forty-eight hours required for contraceptive safety...

That night, with the kids in bed, when she sat alone at the table with Bowie, he asked her what was up with her.

"Up?" she replied, so calmly, so innocently. "I don't know what you mean."

"You seem...different."

"Different, how?"

"I don't know. Like you've got some big secret, I guess."

"A bad secret?"

"How would I know—unless you want to share it with me?" He gazed at her coaxingly.

She tried not to stare at his mouth, not to think about kissing him. "There's nothing, really."

"You sure?"

"Positive."

* * *

The next morning, she took another pill. And then another the morning after that.

And then, all of a sudden, it was Friday.

She got out the pill case and stared at the remaining pills and thought that if she only put the case away now, without taking a pill, she would have the best kind of protection.

Protection against her own foolish desire.

It wasn't too late. She hadn't made her move and she didn't *have* to make a move.

And then, with a surrendering sigh, she popped the next pill free and placed it on her tongue.

That day crawled by. Glory thought more than once that it would never end. Every hour took a lifetime, every minute a year.

Breakfast lasted forever, with Bowie right there, serving up the pancakes, totally unaware of what she intended to try to do to him that night. When that agony of a meal was finally over, when Johnny was off at school and Bowie was out in the shop, Glory cleaned bathrooms and scrubbed floors.

She got down on her knees in the kitchen and washed that floor by hand. Was it something of a penance before the fact? Ugh. Maybe Angie was right and she was getting to be a lot like Aunt Stella.

But then again, why would Stella need to do penance—before the fact or otherwise? Stella never sinned.

Glory met Angie at the diner at noon. She got through the entire lunch without telling her sister what she planned to do that night. It did seem to her that Angie looked at her strangely more than once.

But that could have just been her guilty conscience making her overly sensitive.

Back at home, she cleaned some more. She took the dishes down from the cabinets and washed the shelves. She probably would have started washing down walls, but Sera got fussy and she had to spend an hour walking her, singing to her, jiggling her gently, trying to comfort her.

Finally, Sera settled down and Johnny came home from school. She helped him wrap the birthday present he was taking to the sleepover, then sent him upstairs to fill a pack with his pajamas and his toothbrush and everything he might need for a night away from home. She had him put his sleeping bag in the back of her Subaru wagon. Then he had to run out to the shop to check in with Bowie.

Finally, he reappeared. "Bowie says he can either watch Sera or drive me...."

"That would be great if he'll drive you. Your sleeping bag's in the Subaru."

She kissed her son goodbye and started dinner.

Bowie came in at five-thirty. She heard him go into the bathroom next to the laundry room and she heard the shower running. Her hands shook as she cut up the salad. And she almost dropped the pot of boiled potatoes in the process of carrying them to the sink to drain them. A woman in her state probably shouldn't be cooking.

But if she didn't make dinner as usual, Bowie would step in and do it for her. And he would start asking questions about what was the matter.

When he finally came out of the bathroom, she heard him in the laundry room, putting a load in the washer. And then, at last, he appeared, fresh from his shower, totally innocent of her wicked plans for him later that evening.

He set the table. "Kind of quiet around here, without Johnny...."

She fished the fried chicken out of the pan. "Give it a few minutes. Sera will be wailing."

"Smells good."

It was a miracle she hadn't burned the whole meal to a crisp. But she didn't tell him that. He would only ask why and she would be forced to lie to his face or tell him straight-out that she had decided to have sex with him and she intended to do so that very night.

He ate with gusto. The poor guy had no idea what was in store for him. She had some cookies she'd made the day before to offer for dessert. He had coffee with those and he seemed to want to linger at the table and chat.

But then Sera started crying and she said, "She's hungry. I'll see you later."

He got right up and carried his cookie plate and coffee cup to the sink. She left him and went upstairs. Miracle of miracles, Sera ate and had her diaper changed and went back to sleep.

Glory took a bath. She put her favorite apple-scented bath oil in the water and she ran the tap nice and hot. Once settled in the steamy tub, she rested her head on a fluffy towel and tried to clear her mind of things like guilt and second thoughts.

Back in the bedroom after her bath, she got a pair of pink silk panties from her dresser. She was slipping them on when she happened to glance over and catch sight of her wedding picture, of Matteo, looking so happy to have her as his bride.

She went straight to the nightstand and turned the picture facedown. Okay, it was childish and it accomplished

nothing. Still, she just wasn't up for glancing over and
seeing her poor dead husband's smiling face while she
ran around getting ready to put a move on Bowie Bravo.

Again.

After all these years.

She had a nightgown she'd bought on sale the previous
spring and never worn. That seemed the best choice. It felt
wrong to wear something she'd worn with her husband.
The nightgown was white, sleeveless, with little ruffles
down the front and a pink ribbon that tied at the throat.
The material was lightweight cotton. She stood in front
of the mirror and thought that it was pretty, but not sexy.

Which was fine. Great. She was almost thirty, a widow
with two children. She didn't need some sexy nightgown
showing off the extra pounds she'd put on since the last
time Bowie saw her naked.

Naked.

Oh, Lord.

Better not to think that far ahead.

The clock by her facedown wedding picture said
7:27 p.m. It seemed a little early for seduction.

But on second thought, how long did she have until
Sera woke up? A couple of hours, if she was lucky.

So she put on her red velveteen winter robe. She stood
at the mirror on the inside of the closet door and brushed
her hair so it fell in soft waves on her shoulders. And then
she hiked up her robe and her nightgown and took off the
pink panties. She didn't need them. Not to do what she
was about to do.

She pulled on her favorite fur-lined Uggs—again, not
sexy. But she did have to walk across the snowy yard to
get where she was going.

And then she was ready. It was time.

Her heart stuck high in her throat and her pulse racing

like a jackrabbit on the run from the big, bad wolf, she grabbed the baby monitor and headed for the barn. Halfway down the stairs, she almost lost her nerve. But she put one booted foot in front of the other and before she knew it, she was out the back door.

The light was on in the workshop. She breathed a sigh of relief that he hadn't gone off to visit Chastity or one of his brothers.

Quickly, before her courage got away from her again, she raced across the thin blanket of leftover snow to the workshop door. She started to knock.

And that was when she heard the impossible sound coming from inside.

A woman's laughter.

Chapter Ten

The woman inside the workshop laughed again. And she said something. Glory had no idea what. The words were muffled by the workshop door.

Glory stood there in the darkness, clutching the baby monitor in one hand and the collar of her robe in the other, trying to wrap her numb brain around what an idiot she'd been.

A woman. Bowie was in there with a woman....

Really, she'd had no clue. No idea. None. He'd never mentioned that he was seeing anyone. She saw him three or four times a day. Never once had there been mention of so much as a date, let alone a girlfriend.

And no one in town had said a word about his seeing someone. In the Flat, if you were seeing someone, everyone knew it eventually.

Shouldn't she have heard *something*?

And really, what did it matter? It was probably for the best. She didn't need to do this. She *shouldn't* do this.

And now, well, she *wouldn't* do this.

Glory swiped at her cheek with the back of her hand.

Tears. She could not believe it. She had started to cry.

It was too much. She would not stand out here by the workshop door in her nightgown and cry. No. She would go back to the house this very minute. She started to turn.

But she was too late.

She stopped in mid-whirl and stared in horror, rooted to the spot, as the door swung wide.

Fully dressed and wearing boots and a heavy winter coat that failed to disguise her far-advanced pregnancy, Charlene Bravo stood on the other side. "Glory!" Charlene cried in surprise. "Hey, I was just…" Her brow furrowed in concern. "Glory, are you all right?"

Glory sniffed. "Fine. I am just fine." She brushed furiously at her wet cheeks and chirped way too brightly, "So, what's up? How are you doing?"

Charlene patted her big tummy. "Only six weeks to go. I came to see the crib Bowie's made for me." She sighed. "It is so beautiful. A work of art."

"And she brought me a pie." Bowie stood behind Charlene with one of her famous pies held proudly in his big hands. "Blackberry." He looked so pleased. But then he got a better look at Glory's tear-streaked face. His gold brows drew together. "Glory, what's the matter?"

She tried to look relaxed and casual and knew that she was failing utterly. "Not a thing. Just thought I'd…come out and, uh, see how you were doing. With everything. See if you're comfortable and, you know, if you, um…" Oh, God, how lame can you get? She needed to shut up. She needed shut up right now.

Charlene must have noticed that Glory was all bathed and scented and ready for bed, but she didn't say a word about it. "Well, I was just leaving." She kept her voice pleasant and neutral as she dodged around Glory and sent a parting glance in Bowie's direction. "Thank you again."

He nodded. "I'll bring the crib over tomorrow."

She hustled off down the icy walkway that led around to the front of the house. Glory watched her go. It was better than turning and facing the man who stood behind her in the open doorway.

"Come on in," he said softly, once Charlene had disappeared from view.

She didn't turn. She couldn't. Never in her whole life had she felt like such a silly, hopeless fool. She stared hard straight ahead. "Uh, no, really. I'm sorry. I shouldn't have come out here. I'll just—"

"Glory." He touched her shoulder. She felt that touch clear down to her toes. "Come inside."

She made herself face him. "Oh, I don't think that's such a good idea now."

He had the pie in one hand. With the other, he reached out and wrapped his warm fingers around her arm, just below her elbow. "Come on." His voice was so patient, so completely unruffled.

She should have pulled away. He wasn't the wild man he used to be. He wouldn't make a scene or anything. He would simply let go if she insisted more strongly. But she didn't insist. She didn't try and shake him off. She only whispered breathlessly, "Bowie, I..."

He waited, giving her time to finish whatever it was she'd started to say. But words had deserted her. She simply stared at him, bereft. After several endless seconds, he pulled her inside.

He put the pie on the workbench by the door. "Give me the monitor." She obeyed automatically. He took it from her and set it down, too. Then reaching around behind her, he shut the door.

She heard the latch click, heard him press the lock home. It seemed such a final sound. She went weak in the knees. "Oh, Bowie, what am I doing?" she heard herself ask.

He gave her no answer but only instructed, "Come over by the fire...."

"I don't, um..."

"This way." He took her there, to the old parlor stove where the flames burned bright and cheery behind the ceramic-glass viewing window.

She shivered and turned her back to it, felt the heat of it radiating through her robe and nightgown, so toasty and welcome after the chill outside.

He still held her arm. With his other hand, he guided a loose curl of hair back over her shoulders, smoothing it. And then he touched her face, brushing those rough fingers against her tender skin. It felt absolutely lovely, that touch of his. "What happened, Glory? Why were you crying?"

Why did he have to ask that? It only made her throat feel tight and the tears rise up behind her eyes all over again. "It's only that I...well, I... Oh, do we have to talk about it?"

"Come here. Come on..." He led her over to the cot in the corner, and then pulled her down beside him. "Here you go." He offered her a tissue from a little box on the old stool that served as his nightstand.

She whipped one out, dabbed at her eyes and wiped her cheeks. "I'm such an idiot." She balled up the tissue and tossed it in the wastebasket on the other side of the stool. "Just a ridiculous, silly, silly idiot."

"No," he said so tenderly.

"Yes, I am. I truly am. I..."

"What? Why? I don't understand."

She gulped. "I plotted and planned, Bowie. I did. I intended...to seduce you."

Apparently, he'd already figured that out. He didn't look especially surprised. "Well, all right." He said it firmly, as though he approved.

"No," she cried. "It's not all right."

He took her by the shoulders, a steadying sort of touch, and he looked straight in her eyes. "Let me put it this way. It's all right by me."

Her lower lip trembled. She ordered it to be still. "It is?" He nodded. "I'm...glad," she confessed. And then she couldn't look at him. She turned away.

He caught her chin gently, guided it back around to him. "You don't seem very glad."

"Well, that whole thing, just now, with Charlene..."

"What about it? It was no big deal."

"But it was! It was a big deal to me."

He ran those warm palms of his down her arms, and took her hands in each of his. "She's a great person. She cares for both of us. She won't think less of you, if that's what you're worried about. And she's never been one to gossip or spread rumors. That's not who she is."

"You're right. I know you're right, but..."

"But what?"

She pulled her fingers free of his grip. "Oh, it's so stupid..."

"Tell me."

She blew out a hard breath. "I got out here, I was just about to knock on the door, and I heard Charlene laughing inside and I thought that, well, that..." It was all too much. "Oh, never mind what I thought." She just couldn't look at him. She let her shoulders sag and she stared miserably down at the round sheepskin toes of her boots.

"Hey."

"Oh, Bowie…"

"Come here." He wrapped an arm around her and gathered her close. "I get it, okay?" She felt the sweet pressure of his lips on her hair. "You thought I had something going with some other woman."

She buried her head against his chest, which was warm and solid and felt so good to lean on. And she confessed into his shirt, "I did. Yes."

He took her chin and made her look at him. "There's no one. I promise you."

She let out a moan. "I realized that the minute Charlene opened the door. It didn't make me feel like any less of a fool, though."

"You're not a fool."

"Could you say that again?" she asked meekly.

"Glory, you are not a fool."

With a low moan of sheer misery, she turned her head into his hard shoulder again.

He cradled her so tenderly. "You always smell like apples." His voice was suddenly gruff. "You know that?"

"Apple bath oil." She sniffed.

"Apples and rain…"

"I don't know about the rain part."

He chuckled then. "I do."

She snuggled in even closer. "I'm just a nervous wreck. All this scheming and planning. It can really wear a girl out.…"

He tipped her chin up again. "You've been scheming and planning?"

"Didn't I just say that a few minutes ago?" She blew a wild strand of hair out of her eyes.

Tenderly, with a finger, he smoothed that strand of hair back into place. "For how long?"

"Weeks." She rolled her eyes. "Men are so clueless."

"Maybe so."

"Hmm. No 'maybe' about it."

He touched her cheek with the back of his hand, his gaze soft and tempting as a hazy summer morning. "Give me a break, will you? Until I saw you standing outside that door in this pretty red robe, I was still operating on the agreement we made after I kissed you. You do remember that kiss?"

She gazed up at him and sighed. "How could I ever forget?"

"Glory." He brushed her lower lip with his thumb, so gently, back and forth. "You hardly spoke to me for a week after that kiss."

"I know. I'm…well, I'm sorry, okay? If I'm giving crossed signals."

His gilded brows drew together. "And I'm sorry, too, but I have to ask…"

"Oh, God, what?"

"While you were planning and scheming, did you happen to maybe pick up a box of condoms?"

"No, but there's no need to worry. I'm, uh…" She came out with it. "I'm on the pill."

All at once, his eyes were shining. "On the pill, huh?" He framed her face between his hands. "Now that's the way to plan and scheme."

"Oh, Bowie…" Her heart had set to racing again. And a thousand overactive butterflies seemed to have taken up residence in her stomach.

He framed her face with both hands. "You're shaking."

She leaned closer, whispered fervently, "Just kiss me, okay? Just kiss me and everything will be all right."

"Just kiss you…"

"Yes, kiss me. Kiss me now."

He gave her what she asked for. Light as a breath, his

mouth settled over hers. His lips were so warm, so tender. So fine. She sighed in delight.

And with slow, deliberate care, he deepened the kiss.

In the stove, a log shifted, settling. Other than that, the workshop was quiet. And from beyond the walls of the old barn, she heard nothing. As though the night itself had gone silent, breath held, waiting.

And all at once, she was aware of her own breathing. It sounded a little ragged, a little scared. But eager, so very eager.

She opened her mouth to him and his tongue slid over hers, tasting her. She moaned, it felt so good. The sound echoed inside her head.

He lowered one hand, so slowly, skimming the side of her neck, raising goose bumps as he went. And then his mouth followed where his fingers had been. He kissed his way downward, following the path blazed by his touch—and then he lifted his head to claim her mouth for a second time.

She accepted his kiss with enthusiasm, opening, inviting him inside.

He took what she offered. And as he kissed her so deeply, his fingers strayed. He molded the shape of one shoulder, traced the deep vee at the collar of her robe.

His intention became clear a second later. He tugged on the end of the sash at her waist. The robe fell open.

He slipped his hand inside to clasp her waist. Her breath got all tangled up in her throat at the stunning intimacy of that simple touch. There was only the light barrier of her cotton nightgown between his palm and her bare flesh. "Glory..." He kissed her own name onto her lips.

She moaned a little. How could she help it? He pushed

the robe off her shoulders, down her arms. She did the rest, wriggling out of it, eager to be free of it.

He took it from her, urging her to lift up because she was sitting on the bottom half of it. Once he had it out from under her, he tossed it toward the easy chair by the fire.

Cradling her cheek in a tender hand, he broke the long, deep kiss. "So pretty…"

Her eyelids felt heavy, weak with desire. But she opened her eyes anyway. She wanted to watch the emotions play across his face as he carefully untied the little pink bow at the top of her nightgown.

He bent close and pressed his lips to the base of her throat. She gasped when he did that. And he put out his tongue and tasted her skin.

"Oh, yes. Like that…" She needed him closer. She reached out and gathered him into her, pressing his golden head to her breasts.

He found her nipple through the nightgown and scraped it lightly with his teeth. The feeling was so intense, like a cord pulling tight between her breast and her womb.

She caught his face, made him look at her. "Careful. My milk will come.…"

He surged up and captured her mouth again, his hand cradling her breast, but lightly. With exactly the care she'd asked for.

So strange and forbidden—and wonderful, too, to be with him this way.

Again. After so long.

He was so different. So careful and gentle.

Different, and yet just the same. The heat of his body, the feel of him in her arms. So well-remembered.

Like coming home.

He guided her down onto the cot, and then rose up above her. He eased himself between her knees, and pushed her nightgown high on her thighs.

"Beautiful," he told her. "You're so beautiful, Glory. Just the way I remembered. But better. More..."

She tried to reach for him again, to bring him down to her, to capture his lips and kiss him forever. But he only shook his head and clasped her thighs. He caressed her knees, rubbing the backs of them, where the skin was most sensitive. He cupped her calves in either hand, massaging them, so that she moaned at the feel of his strong fingers, kneading the tension away, knowing just where to press, just how to rub.

He lifted one leg across his lap and pulled off her boot and then he did the same with the other. Once her feet were bare, he kissed her toes. All ten of them. One by one.

She giggled and sighed. He laughed low in his throat as he took one of her legs and eased it wider, guiding it around him, so that he was between her knees once again. He bent over her. She gazed up at him, into those shining blue eyes.

And at that moment, in the tiny cot by the old stove, she felt achingly young again. Young in a way she hadn't felt since the day she first realized she was pregnant with Johnny.

Young. Carefree. Perfectly happy to follow the insistent demands of her yearning body, her hungry heart. Without stopping to think. Without worrying about consequences. Without fear for the future.

It was her ultimate forbidden fantasy. To be with him, in this special, intimate way again. It didn't seem possible that it had actually happened, that it was real. Right now. Tonight...

She had given him up along with her youth, turned her back on the memory of him, of *this*—so very long ago.

Yet it *was* real. It was happening.

His mouth was there above hers, for the taking. And she did take it. She drew him down until his lips touched hers. The feel of him was so good.

So very right.

With the tip of her tongue, she traced his mouth, teasing at the seam between his lips. And when he let her inside, she tasted him as deeply as he had tasted her.

So good. Yes. She had forgotten *how* good, had made herself forget. For so many reasons.

For her own emotional survival. For the sake of her dear, lost husband—and yes, in a sort of pointless revenge for the long, empty silence this blue-eyed bad boy had put between his heart and hers.

She had purposely forgotten this splendor, this wonder—until the moment she saw him again, coming out of the storm the day her daughter was born. That day, in spite of everything, she had felt desire stirring.

But the specifics remained lost to her.

Until tonight.

Tonight, her eyes were open again. Tonight, she reclaimed every last sweet, ecstatic memory.

The memories belonged to her. As *he* belonged to her.

"Your shirt," she demanded, "take it off." She worked at the buttons. And when they didn't part fast enough, she sent a few flying. One pinged against the stove. She laughed low in her throat at that and pulled his shirttails free of his jeans.

Finally, he helped her. He lifted away a little and fumbled to get the sleeves down his arms. So much for the shirt.

Next came his jeans. She undid the buttons, opened his

fly and pushed them down—along with his boxer briefs, both at the same time.

"Always in such a hurry..." He breathed the words against her throat. "Not that I'm complaining...."

"Get these jeans off."

He didn't argue. He knew better. Between them, they managed to get the jeans down. He'd already kicked off the moccasins he was wearing, but still, in the end, he had to pull away from her and sit on the edge of the cot to get the wadded-up denim past his ankles and off.

She lay back on the pillow and gazed her fill at him, not even caring that her nightgown was all in a bunch at her waist. Unabashed, she stared at him. He was so fine, even with all the scars from the years when he just had to fight any fool who looked at him crossways. His chest was so beautifully sculpted, his belly ridged and flat. His arms were even harder and thicker than she remembered. His hips were so lean, his thighs and legs corded with sharply defined muscle....

He looked over at her, a look that burned her, although his lips curved in a wry kind of smile. There was no doubt of how much he wanted her. He was so hard, so ready.

She couldn't resist. She came off the pillow, reaching for him and wrapped her fingers around him.

He groaned at that.

She gathered her knees under her and lowered her mouth to him, tasting him, first with her tongue in long, slow strokes. And then all the way, taking him deep.

He speared his fingers through her hair, clasping, lifting his hips to her as she took him all the way inside—and then, with slow, delicious care, let him out again.

That didn't last long.

He tugged on her fisted hair—gently but urgently.

"Enough of that." His voice was rough with need. "You'll push me right over the edge...."

She sat back on her heels and slanted him a lazy look. "That was pretty much my plan."

"You and your plans..."

"You said you weren't complaining."

"And I'm not. No way." He still had one hand in her hair and he opened it, spreading his fingers wide to cradle the back of her head. He pulled her closer until a feather couldn't be slipped between her mouth and his. "Glory Ann?"

"Um?"

"You have no panties on."

"You noticed." She smiled against his lips.

"I did. The sight gives me...great pleasure."

"Good." She kissed him. She couldn't get enough of that, of her mouth meeting his. The taste of him thrilled her. And he smelled of the pines and the wind in the spring.

And when he guided her back down to the cot again, she went without hesitation. She still had her nightgown on, but so what? He pushed the light fabric out of his way and he caressed her breast with a careful, light touch—so knowing, so achingly tender.

He made her crave more from him. He made her want everything he could give her—every touch, every kiss, all of it. Now. He stroked the flesh over her ribs and lower, his fingers gliding into the cove of her waist and on down. He caressed the side of her hip.

She couldn't wait. She was on fire. For more. For all of him. Reaching down, she took his hand and guided it over the top of her thigh....

And inward. He petted the dark curls where her thighs met. And then he did what her aching body was begging him for. She moaned long and low when he touched her most secret places. Already, she was wet and slick for him. Wanting him.

Yearning...

Finally, he guided her thighs apart and he settled himself between them.

She lifted her hips to him—and he slid home.

Stars exploded. Time hung suspended. Her body gave around him, welcoming him. She sank her teeth into his shoulder at the stunning sensation, at the sheer erotic wonder of having him within her again.

He pressed in even tighter. And then he lifted up on his elbows and gazed down at her, eyes gone dark as the blue at the bottom of the sea.

"Glory..."

"Yes." She tossed her head on the pillow, lifted her body up to him. "Oh, Bowie. Yes..."

"I like that word. You should say it more often."

"Yes. Yes, yes, yes..."

He began to move inside her. She lifted her legs and wrapped them around him and let him carry her away.

Into the heart of her own pleasure. Into the absolute center of the fire.

Chapter Eleven

Glory woke to the sound of her baby crying.

She opened her eyes and found Bowie, lying on his side next to her, his head braced on his hand. Watching her.

He kissed the tip of her nose. "I was just trying to figure out how I could go get her without waking you up."

"Not possible. This cot's too small." She could feel his every movement, every slightest shift.

Sera let out an angry screech.

"I'm on this." He was already levering up and climbing over her, all sleek muscles and easy grace. She had to admit, it was a great view. He landed on his feet by the side of the cot. "I'll bring her out to you...." She tried to sit up, but he pushed her back down. "Stay there." He pulled the covers up over her, tucked them around her in a conscientious way that made her feel cherished. Cared for.

She tried to argue. "It's too cold out there for her...."

"I'll bundle her up nice and warm."

With a sigh, Glory gave in and snuggled back under the blankets. "Bring the diaper bag."

"Don't worry." He shook out his jeans and pulled them on. Then he grabbed a sweatshirt from the ancient chest of drawers on the back wall. He was fully dressed and out the door in less than a minute. Glory shut her eyes. But that was pointless. Sera was wailing her heart out. That little girl could wake the dead when she really got going.

But then, from the monitor on the workbench, she heard Bowie. "Hello, beautiful…" The baby quieted instantly, as she always seemed to do at the sound of his voice. "Come on, now," he told her. "Your mamma's waiting for you…." Sera made the sweetest little cooing sound. "What did you do with that diaper bag? Ah, here we go…."

After that, there was silence. Glory pushed back the covers and reached for her robe. She was just knotting the sash when he brought Sera in.

She sat in the rocker on the far side of the stove and he handed the baby to her. Sera latched right on and started nursing. Glory rocked gently and thought how peaceful and contented she felt.

How, until right now, she hadn't felt any kind of peace, not in months and months.

Not since Matteo died.

Matteo.

Just thinking his name brought reality sharply, painfully back.

Bowie had picked up his whittling. He sat in the old horsehair easy chair on the other side of the stove, the wastebasket between his moccasins to catch the shavings, as he carved swiftly and expertly at a small piece of wood.

Glory stared at his golden head, which was bent to his work. *What have I started?* she fretted. *How will it end?*

As if he sensed her gaze on him, Bowie tipped his head and met her eyes. It was all there in that blue gaze, everything that had happened that night.

The way she had come to him, the comfort he had offered her when she cried—and the pleasure they had shared, too.

He said, so gently, "I'm glad that you're here tonight."

She spoke around the sudden lump in her throat. "We have to be…careful."

He almost smiled. But his eyes were suddenly so somber. "Careful, huh?"

"There's Johnny to think about."

"Right. Johnny."

"He's a little kid. He wouldn't understand."

He put the wood and the knife on the table beside him. "You don't know that."

The sweet peace she'd been enjoying before had evaporated. Annoyance sizzled along her nerve endings. "Of course I know. I'm his mother."

He bent, picked up the wastebasket and set it to the side. "So, then. You didn't think about Johnny while you were plotting and scheming on how to get in my bed?"

She hardly knew what to say to that. Grudgingly, she confessed, "I did think of him, yes. But maybe not as much as I should have."

His big shoulders slumped as he let out a long, wearysounding breath. "Okay, let's do this. Why don't you tell me how you want to handle this, with us, and I'll tell you if what you want can work for me?"

She looked down at her baby, who was nursing so sweetly, and then back up at the man who waited for some kind of answer from her—the man who deserved an answer, she knew that. She said it straight out. "I don't want to tell anyone. I want to keep this thing strictly between the two of us."

He laughed then. It was not a cheerful sound. "You've got to be kidding. Have you forgotten that we live in New Bethlehem Flat?"

"No one has to know. If we keep it low-key."

"Low-key." He shook his head. "What you mean is you want us to sneak around to see each other."

She longed to deny that. However, what he'd just described, as low and cowardly as it sounded, was exactly what she meant. "It's nobody's business what we do in private."

"No, it's not. And if somebody in this town asks me what goes on between you and me, I'll tell them it doesn't concern them and I'll say that straight out. But sneaking around to be with you, Glory? That's lying, pure and simple."

"It's not...."

"It is. I spent a lot of years lying to myself. About how I was going to change. How I would do better—whatever the hell 'better' actually means. How I wouldn't take another drink or get in another fight. How I'd find a job and keep it. I had to learn to give up the lies first of all before I could even start to get sober and stay that way."

"Bowie." She spoke with care. She did hope to get him to see her side of it, to understand. "I...well, I know I've been hard on you since you came back."

"That's okay." He sounded sincere. "You had a right to be hard on me, if anyone did. I've got no issue with the way you've treated me. You've been fair to me, Glory. More than fair."

"Well, I just want you to know that I admire what

you've done, how far you've come and how well you're doing now. But this is not about your staying sober."

"Oh, come on, you're a smart woman. I think you have to know that everything I do is about my staying sober."

The trouble was, she got what he meant. She understood exactly. And she knew he was right. She came straight out with it. "I'm a coward, okay? A big, fat chicken. I just…I don't want to get my son upset and I don't want the whole town talking about how you and I are at it again with Matteo not even a year in his grave."

"If Johnny's upset, we can deal with that—not that I think he will be. And as far as the whole town talking, what does that matter? You loved your husband, I know that you did. But he's gone now. If anybody expects you to spend your life all in black, well, that's their problem, not yours."

She let out a low sound. "You sound just like Angie."

He grunted. "I always did think highly of Angie." And then he rose from his chair and came over to hers. He knelt at her feet, his face tipped up to her, his eyes so clear, his skin healthy and tanned. A good man. An honest one.

Exactly the man she'd always longed for him to be, back in the day when everything was new between them.

She looked down at him and her heart melted. "Oh, Bowie…"

He touched the baby's head, one gentle stroke. And then he reached up and pressed his palm against Glory's cheek. She leaned into his caress, wishing they could just stay that way, by the fire, her baby in her arms and his hand on her cheek. Forever.

But it couldn't last. He took his hand away. "It's what *we* think about what we're doing that counts. And anyway, sneaking around isn't even going to work. Not in this town. Someone will find out. Charlene probably already knows."

"Didn't you say yourself that Charlene won't tell anyone, that she doesn't carry tales?"

"Except to my brother. You know she'll tell Brand."

"And Brand will keep it to himself."

"And Angie. Come on, Glory, you know that Angie is going to find out because you're going to tell her."

"No, I'm not." She knew it was a lie as she said it. And she hated herself for being the liar in this painful conversation. His eyes reproached her. "Okay," she confessed. "Yeah, I probably will tell Angie, but she's my sister. I tell her *everything*. It's different, with her."

"Different, huh? And you know that she's going to tell Brett, right?"

"Will you just…not rub it in, please—and what do you want from me, anyway? You want to come and live in my house with me, sleep in my husband's bed?"

He rose slowly and stood looking down at her. His eyes were shadowed now and his mouth was set. "No. No, I don't want that. It's the last thing I want."

"Then what, Bowie? What *do* you want?"

"I want you to be straightforward. Truthful, the way you've always been. Yeah, what we do when we're alone is nobody's business and I'm good with that. But I'm not going to pretend when I see you in the diner or go to dinner with the family that there's nothing between us anymore, that it's all over and done with us and we're only about doing our best for Johnny. Doing our best for Johnny is important, but it's not everything. Not as of tonight."

"It *is* everything. And it's not the best thing for Johnny if the kids in school start carrying tales about us that they got from their parents."

"If they do, he'll deal with it. He's a hell of a kid with a fine head on his shoulders. You're not giving him enough credit."

"And you're not listening to me."

He blew out a hard breath. "Why can't I ever seem to get through to you, Glory? Someone else, other than Brand and Charlene and Angie and Brett—someone else will see us together and guess what's going on. It's just the way things work around here. It's the way it's always been. You're begging for a big, bad surprise if you actually believe you can carry on a thing with me and no one has to know."

"Because they don't!" She said it too forcefully. Sera popped off her breast and stared up at her, wide-eyed. "Oh, honey, so sorry..." she soothed in a whisper. She turned her around and put her on the other side.

Bowie waited until the baby was settled and nursing again before he said, "I don't like it. I don't like that you want to sneak around to be with me. And I don't like that you actually think no one's going to figure it out."

She knew what they were coming to in this discussion. It was not a good place. And she knew herself to be the dishonest one. It wasn't right, what she was asking of him. She really ought to have more integrity than this.

But she wanted him. So much. She wanted more of what they'd shared on that narrow cot such a short time ago.

She wanted him and she didn't want to upset her little boy or have the whole town whispering behind their backs. And so she persisted, "As long as you're living here, in the workshop, it won't be that difficult to keep what we have to ourselves."

He stared down at her for a long time. And then he said, "For a week, you mean?"

She frowned at him. "A week?"

"I'm closing on the Halstotter place a week from today. After that, I won't be living here anymore."

"A week..." How had she managed to let herself forget how soon he would be leaving?

"That's right," he said. "A week. And as for being careful, for keeping what's going on with us some deep, dark secret? No, I'm not willing to do that, Glory. I'm just not."

And so their beautiful, passionate secret affair was over. Just barely begun.

And over already.

Bowie avoided being alone with her. He still came in for breakfast and dinner. He was polite and he was helpful, as he had been since that first day he returned to town.

But he avoided any chance they might end up alone together. He didn't come across the yard to see her either Saturday night or Sunday after the kids were in bed.

Monday, Glory went to lunch at Angie's house. She told her sister what she'd done with Bowie on Friday night. And then she told her that they'd already ended it—and why.

"Bowie's right," Angie said when Glory finished revealing all. "If you want to be with him, it's wrong that you should make it some back-door affair."

"Angie, could you please not tell me what I already know?"

"Then go to him. Tell him you see how off base you've been and beg him to give you another chance."

"I don't think so. I, well, I just don't think I'm ready for this, for him and me, all over again, you know?"

Angie shook her head. "If you weren't ready, why did you—"

"Please, could you just, you know...not say it?"

Angie wouldn't quit. "It's a valid question."

"I know. And I shouldn't have done that, gone after him like that. I get it. Getting anything started with him was a bad idea."

"I disagree."

"Fine, you do that. Disagree all you want. But it's still my life and I get to run it."

"I never knew *you* to be a coward, Glory."

"Well, surprise, surprise. That's exactly what I am."

"Bowie's moving out, Mom," Johnny announced Tuesday morning at breakfast. "But he's going to live right here in town and I will see him all the time, even go and have sleepovers at his house a lot of times, more than once a week. Right, Bowie?"

Bowie nodded. "That's right." He glanced in Glory's direction. She just happened to be looking at him right then. Their gazes collided.

They both quickly looked away.

Glory swallowed a spoonful of cereal. It felt like a handful of rocks going down. "Well, I'm sure it will all work out fine." She said it cheerfully. Maybe too cheerfully.

Johnny beamed. "I'm going to get a puppy, soon as Bowie moves."

"Oh, are you now?" She slid Bowie another look. He was staring straight ahead, chewing his cereal with great concentration.

"Yes, I am," Johnny crowed. "I can't wait." He looked from her to Bowie and back again, a worried frown creasing his smooth brow. "Bowie said the puppy was okay with you...."

"Yes," she hurried to reassure him. It wasn't his problem if she and Bowie didn't see eye to eye on the concept of how to behave when having a wild, passionate affair. "Of course it's okay. Bowie and I have discussed the puppy." *Back when he was still talking to me.* "The puppy is fine."

"Mom, I've been thinking…"

She smiled at him. He really was the greatest kid. "About what?"

"Maybe Bowie will let you and Sera come and have sleepovers, too. So you won't be lonely when I'm gone to his house." He turned to Bowie. "Bowie, can Mom and Sera come and stay at your house, too?"

Glory sipped her tea. No way was she touching that one. And she didn't have to. Johnny had just lobbed the ball right into Bowie's court. She sent the man a smug glance.

He didn't even flinch. "Absolutely. Your mom and Sera can stay at my new house anytime."

Johnny beamed. "See, Mom? You won't be lonely after all. You and Sera will be there, too."

"We'll see," she said and tried not to look daggers at the man calmly chewing his cereal across the table from her.

"You don't *want* to come and stay at Bowie's?" Johnny asked. He'd always been perceptive well beyond his years. Sometimes she really wished her son could be a tad more oblivious.

"I think probably it's better if Sera and I stay here when you go to stay at Bowie's."

"Why?" Johnny demanded.

Glory's heart sank as she scrambled to come up with the right reply to that dreaded *why.*

And then Bowie said, "Your mom has been very good to me, letting me stay here so that I can get to know you.

She's welcome at my new house anytime. But that doesn't mean she *has* to come. Your mom lives here. And so does Sera. That's just how it is."

"Oh," Johnny said. "Okay." And he picked up his spoon and dug into his cereal again.

Stunned at how exactly right Bowie's response had been—how adult, how calm, how simple, how downright fatherly—Glory picked up her spoon, too. She finished her cereal.

It tasted a lot like humble pie.

That night, she wanted to go to Bowie. Go to him and beg him, as Angie had suggested, to give her another chance.

On his terms. For the world to see.

The incident at the table that morning had shown her a hard truth. Johnny would be just fine if she and Bowie got together. Her son was a well-balanced person with a very strong sense of self. He would be fine, whatever happened—or didn't happen—between her and Bowie.

He had already accepted Bowie fully into his life. He'd loved Matteo and thought of him as a father. The loss of Matteo had been rough. But now he had Bowie. He wouldn't have to grow up as Bowie had, without the steadying hand of a dad.

Glory was so grateful for that.

And she really had to quit using her son as an excuse not to let Bowie get too close. She needed to be braver, stronger, *better* than she'd been so far. And she sure did need to be a lot more truthful.

But then she looked at Matteo's smiling face in the picture on her night table and it just seemed so wrong.

So immeasurably sad.

He had been so good to her, so generous. So true. He'd given her all that he had. And now he was gone.

And what, really, would be left of him if she let even her loyalty to him go? It seemed that once she turned to Bowie fully and honestly, for everyone to see, then it would be as if Matteo had never existed.

Or worse, as if he'd been merely a placeholder in her life. The one who stepped in and helped her get by until Bowie Bravo returned to reclaim his son and stand beside her at last.

Maybe that wasn't true, but it felt that way. So she straightened her wedding-day picture on the night table and climbed into her bed alone.

Thursday morning, after Johnny had left for school and Bowie was out in the workshop building beautiful furniture for rich people, the front doorbell rang. Glory was walking the kitchen floor with Sera at the time. She'd fed her and changed her and still, Sera kept fussing.

Glory carried the crying baby out to the front hall. Sera wailed in her ear as she pulled open the door.

The woman on the other side was tall and slim, with hair the color of a raven's wing flowing like a dark waterfall halfway down her back. She might have walked straight out of the pages of a fashion magazine, all sleek and perfect, with big green eyes and lips that looked like she'd stolen them from Angelina Jolie.

She took Glory in at a glance. And dismissed her just as fast. "Bowie Bravo, please," she said in a thoroughly bored tone of voice.

Sera wailed some more and squirmed on her shoulder. Glory pressed a kiss to her temple and rocked her from side to side, "In the back," she said, catching sight of the red Mercedes waiting at the base of the front walk.

The woman became even more bored, if that was possible. She let out a slow sigh and asked in a tone suitable for questioning the village idiot, "The back of…"

Sera kept wailing. The woman winced at the sound. Glory pointed toward the stone path beside the porch. "Follow that walkway around to the back. There's a barn. Bowie's got a workshop inside."

The woman turned away, dismissing Glory without another word.

Glory shut the door. "Shh, it's all right," she whispered to her baby, as she reminded herself that no way was she running into the laundry room to look out the window over the folding table.

Sera did not shush. And Glory was already heading through the front hall.

She made it to the laundry room just as Bowie's visitor reached the workshop door. Glory stared at that river of black hair, at that perfect rear end as the woman lifted her slim hand to knock.

A moment later, Bowie, in dusty jeans and one of those old chambray shirts of his, the ones that clung so lovingly to his deep, muscular chest, pulled open the door. He smiled at the woman, said something, probably her name.

She let out a glad cry that Glory could hear from all the way in the laundry room.

And then she threw her arms around him.

Her cheeks burning and her hopeless heart twisting painfully under her ribs, Glory spun from the window and went to the kitchen. Sera kept on wailing and Glory kept walking her, into the central hall, up the stairs, into and out of each of the rooms up there. She made a circuit of the second floor, then went downstairs again and started all over on the first.

Finally, an hour or so later, the poor sweetheart wore herself out. Glory put her in her crib and then couldn't stop herself from looking out the master bedroom's bay window.

The red car was gone.

Whatever Bowie and that strange woman had been doing out in the workshop, they'd finished in under an hour—not that it mattered. It didn't. Bowie had his own life and she didn't care in the least if he wanted to have wild sex with some gorgeous bad-attitude rich bitch.

Except that it *did* matter. And she *did* care.

And hadn't she promised herself she would start being more truthful? With herself, first and foremost.

She turned from the window. There was plenty to do around the house to keep her mind off Bowie. She got to work with the vacuum and a can of Pledge. And after lunch, she went over to the hardware store and ran the register until it was time to go pick up Johnny and his cousins from school.

At dinner, Bowie didn't say a word about the woman with the red car. Glory almost asked him. But she knew that no matter how hard she tried to sound merely curious, her real feelings were bound to show. And Johnny was right there, happily pounding down his favorite mac and cheese with ham. It somehow didn't seem appropriate to start questioning Bowie about another woman in front of their son.

That evening dragged on endlessly. And when she finally got both kids quiet in their beds, she went downstairs for her tea and sat at the table for over an hour, hoping against hope that Bowie might come in again for once, wishing that they might sit and talk the way they used to. Not even really thinking about the black-haired woman anymore. Only thinking of Bowie and missing him so.

But he didn't come. And at nine-thirty, she climbed the stairs to bed. As she was brushing her teeth she heard the faint sound of the back door opening downstairs. He must have been waiting for her to go to bed before he came inside.

That didn't surprise her. But it did make her feel even more glum and despondent than she already was.

When she turned off the tap, she could still hear water running. He was having his shower. Glory closed her eyes and hung her head and willed away the image of Bowie, naked, water streaming over his golden head and down his beautiful, powerful body....

She went back to the bedroom and put on her favorite cozy red flannelette pajamas and got into bed. By then, the water had stopped running downstairs.

Faintly, she heard the back door close.

He was gone. Back to the workshop. Another day gone by in which they'd barely spoken.

Tomorrow was Friday, the day he would sign the final papers on his new property. He would move out.

She would see him often. It was a small town and they had family in common. Not to mention that they shared a son. There would be no end of opportunities to run into him.

And very few chances for them to ever really talk. It was only going to get more difficult to bridge this gap she'd put between them.

She sat up, turned on the lamp, saw her husband's dear face in the nightstand photo—and knew she had yet to give herself permission to move on, to openly and proudly love another man.

To love Bowie...

Not that she was sure Bowie even wanted to be loved by her at this point. Maybe he had that black-haired woman out there in the shop with him tonight....

No, she knew he didn't. She couldn't have said exactly how she knew, but she did. The other woman was only a distraction, someone for her to focus her frustration and anger on, someone for her to blame.

The real issue, the thing that kept her up nights and made her days a misery, was that she hated the idea of him moving to his new place without the two of them coming to some sort of peace with each other.

There wasn't a lot of time left to find that peace. If she didn't make an effort, she could miss her chance. He would be gone. When he lived someplace else, it would become even harder for her to go to him, to talk to him privately.

She had to make a move and she had to make it soon.

Glory pushed back the covers and reached for her robe.

Chapter Twelve

When he heard the knock at the workshop door, Bowie considered not answering it. He was afraid it might be Fiona. She'd said she was driving straight to Reno and catching a flight back to New York.

However, you just never knew with Fiona. She changed her mind as often she changed her shoes. He didn't feel up to dealing with her a second time in a twenty-four-hour period.

But what if it was Glory?

It didn't seem likely. Since she'd left him Friday night to his blackberry pie and his empty cot, she hardly seemed to be able to look at him. And she only spoke to him when it was absolutely necessary.

Still, he had to know.

He shoved back the blankets, pulled on his jeans, stuck his feet in his mocs and went to answer.

The sight of her sucked all the breath from his lungs.

She stood in the halo of light from the back porch, clutching the top of her red robe together, her hair loose and a little tangled, shining on her shoulders. He'd always loved the color of her hair: dark as coffee, but coffee streaked with butterscotch.

"Um, I was…" Her velvety cheeks flamed pink. Why? Because she'd come out here to where he slept when she should have been in her own bed? Because he hadn't finished buttoning his pants and he didn't have a shirt on? He didn't know nor did he care. All that mattered was that she was standing there. She tried again. "I was hoping we might talk a little?"

"Sure." He stepped back, gestured her inside and shut the door as soon she cleared the doorway. She went straight to the stove. He used the moment when she had her back to him to take care of that last button at the top of his fly.

She turned to him. Her sweet mouth trembled. And then she opened it—and a flood of words came pouring out. "Since Friday, we'vd hardly spoken and I…oh, I don't know, you'll be leaving soon and I want us to, well, I guess, be friends, at least. I want you to know that I do realize I've been the dishonest one in this whole thing since you came back. I keep telling myself I'll be more truthful and then, somehow, I'm not so truthful after all— like today when that woman showed up and I told her how to find you out here and then I told myself I wasn't going to run to the laundry room and spy on you through the window in there. But I did, I ran in there with Sera screaming in my arms and stood there, rocking my poor little baby, watching that woman throw herself at you. I hated that, hated to see her hands on you, even though I knew I had absolutely no say in whether you might be kissing some bitchy black-haired woman in really great clothes. I had no say about anything when it came to you because I had walked away from you Friday and that was it for you and me...." She had to pause for a breath right then.

He saw his chance and seized it. "I wasn't kissing Fiona, Glory."

She swallowed, hard. "Fiona. That's her name?"

"Yeah, Fiona Sedgeman. She's a customer. A very good customer. And sometimes she's a pain because she's such a man-eater, but there's nothing going on between her and me."

"Nothing?" She sounded breathless.

"Zip."

"Oh, okay." She almost smiled, but then she seemed to catch herself—and scowled instead. "Not that it's any concern of mine."

He said, very gently, "Cut the crap, Glory."

She winced, but then she nodded. "Yeah, you're right." A small, embarrassed laugh escaped her. "I seriously need to cut the crap, but I seem to be having some real trouble doing that."

He wanted to reassure her. He wanted to take her in his arms. He wanted a whole lot of things that he was unlikely to get. "Look, it's okay. If you want to be just friends, well, we can work with that. We can—"

She let out a soft cry. "Oh, damn you, Bowie Bravo. You know I want a whole lot more from you than friendship. But it's just that I...well, it feels all wrong to me. To forget Matteo so easily, to turn my back on his memory, on everything he and I had and all he was to me..."

"Matteo." He said her dead husband's name carefully. "Not Johnny."

"No." Her big eyes held his. They begged for his understanding. "I see now, I do. Johnny's okay, just like you said. He'll be all right with it, however things work out."

He prompted, "And it's not what people in town will say, not what they'll think about you?"

"Uh-uh, it's me. It's what *I* think. And I think…I feel like I'm betraying my husband every time I look at you." A sad little laugh escaped her. "Which really says a lot about me, huh? I mean, because I did a lot more than just look at you on Friday night. Because I *still* want to do a lot more than look at you.…"

But she wouldn't. He could see it in her eyes. What the hell was it about life? Why did it always have to be so damn unfair? "How am I supposed to fight a dead man, Glory?"

"You're not. Of course you're not."

He fisted his hands at his sides and then forced his fists to open. It always helped when he wanted to punch something to remember that the choice was his. He didn't have to be ruled by the heat of the moment.

"You're angry." Her mouth was trembling again.

Start with honesty, son, Wily always used to say. *The truth is where all the important stuff begins.* "Yeah, I'm angry, but I'm not going to start breaking things. I'm not that guy anymore."

The sheen of tears made her eyes gleam like polished amber. "I know you're not. You're…good, Bowie. A truly good man."

It was too much, standing there apart from her.

All the years he'd kept himself apart from her. And now he was finally ready to be the man she needed. Finally he'd broken free of the drinking, of the never-ending need to take on all comers with his two fists. He'd found work. Good work at which he excelled. He'd returned home and discovered he wanted to stay there. He'd earned the trust of the son he'd left behind. And every time he held Glory's baby in his arms, he felt like a million bucks. He wanted to be something like a father to that little girl. He wanted that a lot.

And best of all, *most* of all, there was Glory. Or so he'd let himself believe there for a few magical hours on Friday night. He'd let himself hope that he finally had a real chance with Glory. He'd given her up once so she and Johnny could have a shot at a better life. But now, well, he had something real to offer her. His heart, his sobriety, the honest work of his two hands.

They could make something fine, the two of them. A good life together. A family.

Except that they couldn't. Because Matteo Rossi's ghost stood between them now.

No. No damn way.

He went to her, eating up the space that separated him from her in three long strides.

"Oh, Bowie." She gazed up at him so intently. He saw her love there in her eyes. Saw her yearning, the same yearning he felt every time he looked at her, every time he heard her name.

He took her shoulders. She trembled at his touch but she didn't pull away. He said, "I always thought well of Matteo. I respected him. I *liked* him. And back in the day, I didn't find much to like in most people. You know that, right?"

Wordlessly, she nodded. A single tear got away from her, breaking the dam of her lower lid, sliding down her cheek. "I know."

"But right now, I could almost hate him. He had four great years with you. I never envied him the time he had with you. Until tonight."

"Don't." She said it softly.

"Don't?" He gave the word back to her on a growl. "Don't what? Don't touch you? Don't look at you in the same hungry way that you look at me? Don't kiss you?"

"Bowie." She said his name as a warning.

A warning he refused to heed. He pulled her into his arms.

She resisted, but only for a moment. And then she melted into him, her soft little body going pliant, her mouth lifted up.

He listened to the hot pounding of his blood, to the need that sang inside him, the heat that flared down low. He lowered his mouth to hers and he kissed her.

She kissed him back with a lost little cry, opening to him so he could sweep his greedy tongue inside. Her hands pressed against his heart and then slid up to link around his neck, to pull him even closer. He felt her fingers at his nape, in his hair. He touched her hair, too. He ran his fingers through it, loving the warmth of it, the silky texture of every separate strand.

He wanted to kiss her forever. While he was kissing her, he could almost forget that she refused to be with him.

Not in the real way.

Not in the way that lasts, the way that matters.

In the end, with another cry, she turned her mouth away from his and buried her face against his shoulder. "No," she whispered on a torn husk of breath.

He opened his arms and stepped back from her. She swayed on her feet, and then caught herself and found her balance. He looked down at the crown of her bent head, waiting.

Until, finally, she lifted her chin and faced him, her mouth so soft and red from kissing him, her cheeks hot with color.

"How long?" he asked in a ragged growl. "Until you can let him go, until being with me doesn't have to mean that you're betraying him?"

Those whiskey-warm eyes pleaded for his understanding. "I don't know. I'm so sorry."

He didn't feel all that sympathetic right then. "You really think he would want this, huh? Want you to be alone and unhappy just to be true to his memory?"

"Of course not. Matteo wasn't like that."

"No, he wasn't. You ought to consider that, Glory, while you're turning your back on the future, on what you and I could have together—on what both Johnny and Sera need."

The next night, after Johnny was in bed, Bowie surprised her. He came in and sat at the table with her while she had her tea.

She watched his face across from her and tried not to wish he would kiss her again. But she did wish it. And that made her feel ridiculous and small-minded and pitiful, too. He wasn't there for kissing. She knew that from just looking at him.

He said, "I signed the final papers on the Halstotter place today."

"I'm…happy for you."

"Thanks." He shifted in his chair. "I'm moving out tomorrow."

She felt slightly dizzy and then realized she'd forgotten to breathe. She sucked in a big breath and let it out in a rush. "Well, all right."

"I wanted to touch base with you before I go."

"Touch base," she echoed. "Of course."

He pushed a small square of paper across the table at

her. "My new phone number at the house. I got lucky and managed to get them to install it today."

"Great." She took the paper, got up and pinned it to the corkboard next to the phone.

When she slid back into her chair, he said, "And also, I wanted to talk a little about Johnny." Johnny. Her stomach knotted and a headache started pounding at her temples. She resisted the need to try and massage it away. He went on. "I mean, about where we go from here, as parents."

She picked up her tea by rote, lifted it to her lips, took a careful swallow. "I see."

"It's just that there are several things we should start thinking about."

She had a pretty good idea what those things might be. Still, she needed to let him speak for himself. "Such things as?"

"I want joint custody, Glory—no, not right this minute," he reassured her. "You can...take your time about it, get used to the idea. But eventually, in the next year or two, I want you to consider letting me be equally responsible for him. I want us to talk it over with him, so he'll know he can count on both of us as his parents."

The headache squeezed harder. She had a powerful desire to shout at him, to tell him in no uncertain terms that he would never take her son from her.

But then he addressed her fear directly. "I'm not trying to take him from you, Glory. I would never do that. You have to know that by now."

She did know that. And she believed him. What he asked was only fair. Only right. For Johnny's sake. "It's just...it's what you said. Give me time. Let me get accustomed to it. Let's play it by ear for a while. Okay?"

"Absolutely."

She knew there was more. "What else?"

He had his hand on the table. He traced the patterns in the wood as he liked to do. She tried not to remember what it felt like to have that hand tracing other patterns, arousing patterns, on her naked skin. He glanced up at her. "We never talked about his last name. You just...gave him *your* last name when he was born."

She heard a whooshing in her ears. Her own blood, pumping much too fast through her veins. Her mouth tasted of copper. Of defensiveness. Of guilt. She had to force her lips to form the truth. "I shouldn't have done that. I was...bitter. You were drunk all the time and you wouldn't even let me have our baby in peace. You came barging in while I was in labor, demanding that I marry you...."

He nodded. She saw no judgment of her in his eyes. "I was a complete asshat."

Asshat. The word made her laugh—a strangled sort of sound, with more pain than humor in it. "Yes, you were."

"I'm not like that anymore, Glory."

"I know you're not. Not in the least."

"I want my son to have my name."

"And that's...the right thing. I can see that. But you'll give me time, the same as with the custody issue?"

"I will, yes. This is just the first step. You and me. Talking it over. Telling each other where we stand."

"We need to be honest with each other," she told him, although really, she was talking to herself. "To *say* the hard things, to get them out there. Like you did just now."

He blew out a breath. "I'm glad you see it that way."

"I do, Bowie. Even though we're not together, we can... work together. To give Johnny the best possible start in life."

* * *

The next day was a sunny one, warmer than usual for early March.

At breakfast, Johnny announced, "Bowie, I know you have a lot of work to do to get moved and I think you will need my help."

Bowie replied, "I'd appreciate that. I can use all the help I can get—as long as your mom doesn't mind?"

What could she say? "I don't mind at all."

An hour later, Glory saw the moving van pull up in front of the house. Burly moving men got out and went around to the barn to start loading the equipment Bowie had bought back in January.

His personal things weren't a big deal. He could fit them all in his SUV and take them to his new home in one trip. Everything else he owned would arrive from Santa Cruz on Monday, he said.

Johnny went with Bowie out to his new place on Catalpa Way and came running in at lunchtime. He ate a peanut-butter and jelly sandwich and gulped down a glass of milk and reported, "It's a big house that Bowie bought, did you know that, Mom? You can see the river from upstairs and there's already one giant shed that Bowie will use to work in. There will be more buildings, too. And he will have people who come and work with him and also maybe hire some people from right here in town. And the house already has some furniture in it. So Bowie will have a bed and a table and stuff to use until he gets his own things."

"Sounds like it's all working out just great," she said, trying to keep her voice bright and cheerful, reminding herself yet again that she had made her choice and no way was she going to drag around being glum about it.

"There's a room in that house just for me, Mom. It has a bed in it already, too."

"That's pretty cool." She knew where this was going. It hurt. A lot. She steeled her heart against the pain and focused on the happiness she saw in her son's eyes.

"Uh, Mom?"

"Hmm?"

"I was wondering if maybe I could stay over at Bowie's tonight? You think that would be okay? Would you miss me too much?"

"I will miss you a whole lot. And yes, if Bowie says it's all right, you can stay at his house tonight. Just tell him to get you home by noon tomorrow."

"Sweet." He got up and ran around the table to hug her. "Thanks, Mom." He smelled of peanut butter and sunshine. She tried not to hug him too hard, and then forced herself not to hold on when he pulled away.

"You think Mom and Sera are missing us?" Johnny asked that night when Bowie tucked him in bed.

Bowie took the coward's way out of that one. "What do *you* think?"

Johnny smoothed the sheet down a little and folded his hands on his stomach, outside the blankets. "Well, I think Sera prob'ly doesn't even know that we're gone. Maybe if she gets crying, she will miss you 'cause you are the one who can make her feel better. But Mom, well, yeah. I think she misses us. But she wants to give us our time to be together. Mom's a good mom."

"Yeah." His throat felt tight. "She's an excellent mom. The best."

"Bowie?"

"Yeah?"

"When I'm real quiet up here in this room, I can hear the river. Can you?"

"Yes, I can."

"It sounds like a friendly giant. Breathing."

"It does, yeah. It really does."

"The river's by my mom's house. How come I can't hear it in my room there?"

"It's deep in a canyon by your mom's house. I'm guessing the sound doesn't travel as well. Plus, your room's in the back there. The walls of the house block sound, too."

Johnny seemed to consider that explanation. "Well, I *like* to hear the river. I *like* this room."

"Good. A guy should like his room."

"And I've been thinking, Bowie. I've been thinking that because you really are my dad, I should maybe call you dad. You think?"

It was a big moment. One of the best moments. "I think that would be great. I would love it—if that's what *you* want to do."

"Well, there was still my other dad, wasn't there?" Those eyes that were so much like Glory's eyes gazed up at him, worried. Shadowed with doubt. Time was an ocean, especially to a kid. An ocean you floated away on. It got harder and harder to recall the geography of faces you didn't see every day. It was eight months since Matteo's death. To Johnny, it must feel like a lifetime.

"Yes," Bowie said, "there was your other dad. He was a very good man and he loved you so much."

Johnny turned his head on the pillow and peered at Bowie sideways. "Did you know him?"

"I did. Not real well, not like you did. But he was always kind to me. And he always said hi whenever I saw him."

Johnny was looking straight at him now. "I'm glad you came back, Bow—Dad."

"So am I. Very glad."

"I don't want you ever to go away again."

"I won't. Not for very long anyway. Sometimes I have to go places for my work. You know that, right?"

Johnny gave a swift, eager nod. "Sometimes maybe I could come, too."

"Yeah. We'll talk it over with your mom. And now and then, when you don't have school, maybe you can."

"But you live here now," Johnny insisted. "You're staying here. In this house, where we can hear the river."

"That's right." Bowie bent close to brush a kiss on his son's smooth cheek. "I'm staying here. I live here. This is my home now." It felt good to say it.

Really good.

What was it Glory had said when he asked her why she'd returned to their hometown?

I'm from the Flat. It's a lot of who I am.

Well, it was lot of who he was, too. And he was glad to be back.

He turned off the light and paused in the doorway to say good-night to his son.

"'Night, Dad."

He was halfway down the stairs when the phone started ringing.

Glory. Her name exploded in his mind like a bottle rocket on the Fourth of July.

Could it be?

He tried not to hope but he couldn't help it.

He flew down the final few steps and grabbed the extension on the table by the newel post. "Hello?"

"So, then." Ma's voice. Hope shriveled to dust and ashes. "You moved. That was fast."

He sank to the bottom step. "I couldn't live in Glory's barn forever."

"Glory with you?"

"Come on, Ma, you and I both know that's never going to happen."

She was quiet for a moment. "She turned you down." It wasn't a question.

He started to deny it, but why lie? "Yeah. She doesn't feel right about being with me. She still loves Matteo."

"She said that?" Chastity demanded sharply.

"Not exactly, but that was what she meant."

"What *exactly* did she say?"

"Sheesh, Ma. Nosy much?"

"Tell me."

For some unknown reason, he did just that. "She said she felt that being with me was a betrayal of Matteo and she just couldn't do that."

"She couldn't, huh?" His mom sounded strange.

"Ma, what's up? You sound seriously pissed."

"I do? Must be a bad connection."

"Ma…"

"Things with Johnny?" Her voice was softer, the anger he'd heard a moment before vanished as though it had never been. "They're good?"

"Things with Johnny are excellent. He's staying the night."

"I'm so glad." She was smiling. He could hear it in her voice.

They talked for a while longer, about his new place, about his plans for moving most of his business to the Flat.

After they said goodbye, he got out his whittling.

While he worked, he tried not to think about Glory. To wonder how she was doing, alone at home, just her and Sera....

There had been better nights, Glory thought as she walked the floor with Sera, who was wide awake and fussing, the same way she did a whole lot of nights. Sometimes Glory worried about her baby. Was there something more going on with her than colic?

But Brett had reassured her that Sera was just one of those kids. A more sensitive kid, whose digestive system acted up a lot. All Glory had to do was to be patient and keep nursing her. Sera's system would catch up and she would grow out of this fussy phase.

Patience, right. Most of the time Glory felt like her patience was at the frayed end of a very short rope.

But at least there was nothing really wrong with her baby. Glory tried to take comfort in that.

And she tried not to long for Bowie. How pitiful was that? His first night in his new house and she was already desperately missing him. Even if she couldn't let anything really meaningful happen between them, at least when he was around, she could see him every day, talk to him now and then....

And hand him the dang baby when she couldn't take it anymore.

It was after five when Sera finally wore herself out. By then, Glory could hardly keep her eyes open. She fell across her bed and sleep sucked her down hard and fast.

She woke to bright morning sun and the sound of the phone ringing. Muttering bad words under her breath, she groped for the phone and put it to her ear. "What?"

"I thought you were meeting us for early mass." It was Angie, sounding disgustingly cheerful.

Glory forced her eyes open long enough to look at the clock. She'd been asleep for four and a half hours. And she was supposed to have been at church with her family at eight. "Ugh. Sera was up all night, which means *I* was up all night."

"Say no more. I understand."

"Can I go back to sleep now?"

"Bowie all moved out?"

"Do we have to talk about this right this minute?"

"You miss him. I can tell by your voice. You should—"

"Can I go now? Please?"

"Chastity wants to talk to you."

"Fine. Great. And you think maybe she could just tell me that herself? But later. Much later."

"I saw her on Main Street, on the way home from church. She asked how you were doing and said she needed to have a little talk with you. It all sounded very mysterious to me."

"Mysterious. Great. Whenever. Except not right now. Right now, I want to go back to sleep until Sera wakes up."

"Sleep tight."

"Hah. Yeah, right." Glory hung up before Angie could start talking again.

She flopped back on the pillows, yanked the covers over her head again...and realized she was suddenly wide awake. With a moan of sheer frustration, she jumped from the bed, pulled on her rattiest robe and went downstairs to get some breakfast.

The kitchen was empty. No Johnny chattering away a mile a minute. No Bowie at the cooktop, her favorite hunky breakfast-making man. Just Glory in her old blue robe, considering whether to go all the way and have bacon and eggs or if maybe it was more of a Froot Loops kind of morning.

She settled on the Froot Loops. Lots of bright colors. Cheerful. Today, she needed all the cheerful she could get. She was just pouring the cereal into her bowl when the doorbell rang.

Bowie.

Can a heart dance? Hers felt like it was dancing.

Could it be? Was it possible? Maybe he'd brought Johnny over, maybe he was going to cook breakfast today after all, because he knew she would feel low, and he couldn't just leave her alone with her Froot Loops waiting for the baby to cry....

But then her dancing heart sank. She knew it wasn't him. She'd made it more than clear that she wanted him to keep his distance, that she wasn't going to let anything further happen between them.

She drooped all the way to the front door.

It was Chastity, looking wide awake and disgustingly alert. "Yep, I have a morning off. My four guests at the B and B left *before* breakfast. Is that coffee I smell?"

"No, but I can make you some." Glory led her back to the kitchen and loaded up the coffeemaker.

"You look like a victim of enhanced interrogation," Chastity said.

"I was up all night with Sera. And yeah, I'm beat." As the coffee brewed, she went to the fridge to get the milk for her cereal. "Angie said you wanted to talk to me."

"Life is short," said Chastity briskly. "And at the end of it, you die."

Glory poured the milk into her bowl. "I noticed that."

"I know you sent Bowie away." It was an accusation.

"Yeah." Glory kept her voice noncommittal because she really did not want to get into it. She put the milk back in the fridge, took her chair and spooned a big mound of bright cereal into her mouth.

Chastity watched her. "So, then, you really don't get the meaning of what I said a minute ago."

Glory swallowed the mouthful of sweet cereal and milk. "Okay, Chastity, what's this about?"

"If you really understood how short life is, if you really got that it can end out of nowhere like it did for Matteo and you don't get a do-over no matter how much you regret the big, fat mistakes you made—"

Glory was becoming annoyed. "If, if and if, *what?*"

"I'm only saying *if* you understood all the things I just said, you would not have sent Bowie away for the second time."

Glory's spoon clinked against the bowl as she dropped it. "What do you mean for the *second* time? You can't lay his leaving town and not coming back for almost seven years at my door."

Chastity sighed. "Well, all right, I'll give you that. He needed to leave you that first time. He had things to learn and he had growing up to do and he just couldn't seem to make any progress while he was living here. But this second time? This was *your* choice. Do you deny it?"

Glory really, really did not want to hear this. "Chastity, you know I love you, but—"

Chastity put up a hand. "Don't tell me that this is not my business. It is very much my business. My son matters to me. *You* matter to me. And so does Johnny and that sweet baby sleeping upstairs. My son loves you. You're the only woman he's ever loved. And you love him. You love him *more* than you loved Matteo Rossi."

Heat flooded up Glory's neck. "How dare you say that to me."

"Oh, maybe because it's the truth—and don't go giving

in to that famous temper of yours and getting all worked up to give me a big piece of your mind. I know you loved your husband, too. And you were a fine wife to him. You made that man happier than he ever believed he could be. So you can just stop feeling bad about loving Bowie more. Because the real truth is, you weren't Matteo's first choice, either."

Chapter Thirteen

Glory almost choked. "I...what?"

Chastity got up, got down a mug and filled it with coffee. "Matteo never told you about his first love, did he?"

"I don't...I...but..."

"You are sputtering, Glory Ann. Now you just be quiet for a few minutes and I'll be happy to tell you about the love that Matteo Rossi threw away."

"I don't..." The most bizarre thought occurred to her. "Chastity, are you saying that *you* and Matteo..."

"Oh, dear heavens, no. I've never been the type who goes for men the same age as my own sons—not that I begrudge any woman love wherever she finds it. Besides, I was still waiting for Blake Bravo at the time, even though I knew good and well he was never coming back. That's how smart and pulled-together I was."

"Then who was she?"

"Years ago, when Bowie was in the ninth grade and

you were still little more than a child, I hired a Grass Valley girl to clean rooms in the summer."

Glory waited, round eyed. "Matteo fell in love with her?"

Chastity was not about to be rushed. She put the pot back on the warmer and reclaimed her chair. "Her name was Emma Sand. She was the sweetest girl. And so pretty, with long golden hair and hazel eyes. She had a room in the back at the Sierra Star, the same one you had, Glory, when you worked for me. I don't know how she and Matteo met, but it's a small town. And boys and girls will find each other. He came around often. I know that some nights he was with her, in her room. And every time I saw them together, well, it was the same as when you and Bowie first found each other. There's no mistaking that glow, that…connection, when two people are head over heels in love. It's like a light shining from inside of both of them. They share a glance, and it can blind you, the brilliance of that kind of love."

Matteo. In love with a girl Glory had never even known existed. And making love to that girl in the room that would be Glory's a decade later…

It was too strange. And Glory suddenly wanted coffee, even if she *was* nursing. Just one cup. With a whole bunch of milk in it…

She got up to get a mug as Chastity continued, "Matteo and Emma kept their love affair a secret."

Glory guessed why. "Matteo's mom was still alive."

"I don't like to speak ill of the dead, but facts are facts. Serafina Rossi was about the most self-centered woman I have ever met. She lost her husband when the poor man was barely forty and she grabbed hold of her only son and wouldn't let go. Matteo was a dutiful son. Loyal to the core. He lived in this house with her until the day she died."

"Serafina found out about Emma?"

Chastity nodded. "She made Matteo break it off. He just never could go against her wishes. It was pathetic, it really was."

"And to think, I went and named my baby after her…"

Chastity grunted. "It's a pretty name. Don't blame a name because a mean woman once had it. Plus, Matteo's grandmother was named Serafina, too. *She* was a lovely person."

"And Emma?" Glory leaned back against the counter and sipped her milky coffee.

"She came to me, crying. Told me everything, that she loved Matteo with all her heart, but he loved his mother more. She said she couldn't stay in the Flat any longer, that her heart was broken and she had to go—and to go far, far away. She had a letter for him, for Matteo. She asked me to see that he got it. She was afraid to mail it, for fear his mother would get her hands on it first."

"Did you know what the letter said?"

"No, Emma didn't tell me. I didn't ask."

"Did you give it him?"

"I did. I went into the hardware store one day when he was there alone and handed it to him. He thanked me with tears in his eyes."

"And that was it? That's the story?"

"Not quite. After Serafina died, Matteo came to me. He asked me if I knew how to find Emma."

"He still loved her."

Chastity gave a sad little shrug. "I told him I didn't know where she'd gone. And I really didn't. She'd left no forwarding address. Matteo took off."

"Left town, you mean?"

"That's right. He closed up the hardware store and he was gone for months."

"Looking for Emma?"

"That would be my guess."

"But he never found her...."

"Yes, he did find her."

"But she wouldn't try again with him?"

"I guess you could put it that way. When he came back, he was thinner. And sadder. And alone. He came to see me. He said that Emma had gotten married, that she was happy with her husband and their two little children."

"He was too late."

"Yes, he was." Chastity sipped her coffee. "And later, when he started going out with you, he paid me another visit. He asked about Bowie first. About how he was doing. I told him the truth. That I really didn't know. I knew where to write to him by then, but Bowie had never done a whole lot of writing back. Matteo told me that he was going to ask you to marry him. I kept my peace as to my opinion on that. I knew Matteo was a good man. And I thought that you could do a lot worse. Then he asked that I not say anything to you about the past, about Emma. He said he wanted to tell you about her himself. I agreed to keep his secret."

Glory admitted, "He never did tell me."

"I'd kind of figured as much. And I would have honored my promise to him and never said a word to you about how he went and chose his mother over the woman he loved. But there comes a time when the living need the truth more than the dead need their secrets kept."

"I always thought of Matteo as so...transparent." Glory shook her head. "Shows what I know."

"We all have secrets, Glory. Most of us think that if our secrets were revealed, the world might come to an end. But the world just keeps turning. And eventually, we figure out that other people have their secrets, too. At the core, we're all the same. With our sadness. Our yearning. Our striving. And our blind, foolish hearts. We throw away our own happiness. And then when it's too late, we wonder where it went."

After Chastity left, Glory ate her soggy cereal and stared at the far wall for a while. She felt cast adrift somehow, lost in the tragic story Bowie's mom had shared with her.

Then Sera started crying. Glory fed her and changed her. For once, the little sweetie settled right down. Glory put her on a play mat in the family room and she kicked her feet and waved her arms and giggled at the mobile of bouncing bees and butterflies suspended above the mat. When she dropped off to sleep again, Glory carried her upstairs. She went into her crib without a peep.

Glory did some laundry. She cleaned the house.

Johnny came home at noon, as promised. Glory was dusting the family room when she saw Bowie's SUV drive up. Johnny jumped out and stuck his head back in to say something to Bowie before he shut the door. Then he came running up the front walk, hauling his backpack along with one hand.

As usual, he talked nonstop all through lunch. It was dad this and dad that. Glory smiled to herself. Johnny had finally started calling Bowie the *D* word. Glory realized that was just fine with her.

Better than fine. She was happy. For both of them.

They went to her mother's for an early dinner. The whole Dellazola clan was there, including Nonna and Pop Baldovino, Glory's grandma and grandpa on her mamma's side.

Before they sat down to eat, Rose got Glory off in a bedroom and lectured her for not inviting Bowie. "As far as we're all concerned, that man is one of the family, and if you're not going to ask him to come to Sunday dinner, well, next time I'll just do that myself."

It was the kind of ultimatum that usually had Glory grabbing her children and heading home in a huff. But this time, she only said meekly, "You're right, Mamma. Next time I'll be sure to invite him."

It was almost worth being such a doormat about it, just to see her mamma's mouth drop open in shock at Glory's gentle response.

Because Bowie wasn't there for Johnny to visit before bedtime, he gave his dad a call. They talked for half an hour, which Glory found kind of cute. And then at eight-fifteen, when she finally tucked him into bed, he said, "When can I go stay at Dad's again, Mom?"

Strangely, hearing that question hardly hurt at all. "How about Wednesday night?"

"That would be so sweet."

"You can call him tomorrow and ask him if that will work for him."

She kissed him good-night and went to feed Sera, who was really on a roll with being easy to deal with. The baby ate, cooed and giggled through her diaper change, and went right back to sleep.

Glory watched an hour of television, had her bedtime tea and climbed the stairs to bed.

She fell asleep quickly—and then woke with a start. It was ten minutes of eleven. She'd barely had her eyes closed for half an hour.

But she'd had the strangest dream, a dream of something that had actually happened, something she'd completely forgotten until now. A dream of Matteo, out in the workshop, one evening not too long after they were married.

Glory had come out to call him to dinner. She opened the workshop door without knocking and found him standing at the nearest workbench, a carved wooden box open in front of him.

He glanced over at her with a start. "Glory! You surprised me...." Already he was pushing the contents back into the box, shutting the pretty hinged lid that was carved with a nature scene—a weeping willow and a graceful doe, her slender, delicate head bent to drink from a stream.

Glory had laughed. "Okay, what are you hiding there?"

He laughed, too—a nervous sort of sound. "Just some of my mother's keepsakes."

"Ah." She went to him, kissed him on the cheek. "Dinnertime."

He'd turned and embraced her, kissing her so sweetly. She wondered now if the kiss might have been at least partly an attempt to distract her from the carved box. "I'll just be a minute," he'd said, and turned her by her shoulders, pointing her back at the door.

She'd returned to the house, oblivious to any secret motives, sending him a last warm glance over her shoulder before she shut the workshop door.

The workshop.

After Matteo's death, she'd hardly been out there. Matteo had spent a lot of happy hours puttering around in that half of the barn. The first few months after he was gone, being out there in his special space had made her feel the loss of him all the more acutely. She'd never gotten around to going through all the stuff he kept there, deciding what to save and what to give away.

Was that carved box still out there, tucked away in a drawer or a cabinet somewhere?

She turned on the lamp, pushed back the covers and put on her robe and slippers. Pausing only to grab the baby monitor from the night table, she tiptoed down the stairs.

In the workshop, she flicked on the overhead bulb, put the monitor on the workbench nearest the door—the same one she remembered Matteo standing at that long-ago evening—and she started going through the endless rows of storage drawers.

The second drawer down in the second row of drawers opened only halfway. Glory shut it. Opened it again. The back of the drawer was right there in front of her.

Or was it a false back?

She eased the drawer off its gliders and set it on the workbench.

And there it was, a second compartment behind the first. The pretty carved box waited there, so easy to find once she started looking.

With care, she eased the box out of its hidden space. She set it on the workbench and then, for a moment, didn't quite dare to open it.

Was it wrong to pry into Matteo's secrets now that he was gone? Who was she to invade his privacy? If he'd wanted her to know what was inside the box, he would have shown her.

She sent a little prayer to heaven for his understanding. And then instantly, she felt a kind of peace, a sense of rightness. Where Matteo was now, he didn't need secrets. And she really had no malice toward him. She was only grateful to have known him, to have been the recipient of his tender care at a time when she needed a companion, when she yearned for a good man to turn to in the middle of the night.

It felt right. It felt okay. To take the lid and ease it open.

Inside, she found a curling lock of golden hair tied with a blue ribbon, three photographs and an envelope with *Matteo* written on it in a small, neat hand.

She touched the lock of hair, smoothed the ribbon with care. And she studied the photos, two of a pretty blonde girl perched on the deck railing in the back of the Sierra Star. She had wide eyes and a shy smile. She tipped her head for the camera, flirting so sweetly with whomever had taken those first two pictures.

The third photo was the same girl, standing at the same railing, with Matteo. A Matteo so young that the sight of him brought tears to Glory's eyes. He had his arm around the girl and the look on his face…it was the dazzled, ecstatic look of a man who has everything. A man far gone in love.

Glory stared at that snapshot for a long time. Finally, she set it aside and picked up the envelope.

It was the letter. She knew it before she opened it. The letter Emma had asked Chastity to give to Matteo.

Dear Matt,

I have to go away now. I can't stay here any longer, not without you. I can't sleep in my room now, the room where we were together, where you said you would never, ever leave me. Where you said we would be married, make a family, have the rest of our lives.

Together.

My love, I need a clean break. I need to forget you. I don't know how I will do that, but I'm determined. Some-

how, I will find happiness. I'm not staying in Grass Valley.
I'm not even going to be in California.

I hope someday you can get free of what is holding you
back. No, I'm not going to write down her name. I'm going
to try not to hate her. I only want, in time, for you to find
someone who can make you smile and fill your days with
all the joy I dreamed of giving you.
With all my love, now and forever,
E.

It was well after midnight when Glory returned to the
house. She brought the carved box and its treasures with
her and put it away on the top shelf of the master bedroom
closet. Someday, years from that night, she would give it
to Sera.

When and if the time was right.

And speaking of Sera...

The fussy little whines had started. Glory went to the
baby's room and got her. She fed her and changed her.
Then she carried her down to the kitchen where she put
the water on for tea.

And she picked up the phone.

Bowie answered on the first ring. "Glory?" The sound
of his voice reached down and touched all of her most private, secret places, just the way it always had.

She kissed her baby's soft cheek, smiled as though the
man on the other end of the line could see her. "How did
you know it was me?"

"Who else would be calling me in the middle of the
night?"

"You busy?"

"Are you kidding? I'll be right over."

Glory stood at the front window in her red robe and

slippers, holding her baby, waiting for him. He arrived in no time, the shiny SUV sliding silently to a stop at the curb in front of the house. She went to the front hall and pulled open the door and watched him run up the walk toward her, a big, handsome man in old jeans and a faded chambray shirt. She thought of that day he came back, of the way he'd come toward her, seeming to materialize out of the swirling snow.

His golden hair was curling on his collar now. She liked it that way, longer.

At the door, he hesitated. His eyes told her he didn't yet quite dare to believe. "Glory?" he asked on a breath.

"I love you," she told him, standing right there at the open front door in the light of the porch lamp in the middle of the night. "I always did. I never stopped. I love you…most of all. I felt bad about that. Bad for Matteo. Guilty. But I see now that feeling bad and guilty doesn't change the basic truth. Feeling bad and guilty doesn't really do a thing for anybody. Love is what matters, Bowie. And I love you." She reached out her hand to him.

He took it, those warm, strong fingers closing over hers. "Glory, I love you. Only you. Always…" He came inside then. She stepped back to make room for him. He pushed the door shut with his boot.

Sera made a cooing sound, as if she recognized him.

Glory stared up into his face, marveling. He looked at her the way Matteo had looked at the golden-haired girl in the old photograph. "I'm so glad you're here. Glad you came back to town at last. Glad you…put up with me until I was ready."

He touched her hair, traced a loving finger along Sera's downy cheek. "For you, I would wait forever. Waiting's no fun, but it's better than the alternative. I'll never leave you again, Glory, not while there is breath in my body. I swear it to you."

She went on tiptoe. He bent his head. Their lips met as the baby in her arms made the cutest little giggling sound. The kiss lasted a long time. Glory reveled in it.

And Sera didn't seem to mind.

When he lifted his head, she said, "I'll just put this baby to bed."

"Let me?" he asked, with obvious eagerness.

Glory handed Sera over. He carried her up the stairs. Glory went into the family room and sat on the sofa, waiting for him.

When she heard his footsteps on the stairs again, she called to him softly. "In here…"

He came and stood above her. His eyes were blue fire. "How many times did I ask you to marry me, back in the day when you kept saying no?"

"I don't remember. So many times…"

"Well, I'm asking again. Marry me."

"Yes," she replied without hesitation. "Yes, yes, yes."

"Right away," he demanded.

She nodded. "As soon as we can get the license."

He bent close, bracing his hands on the back of the sofa, bracketing her between his powerful arms. "That's what I've been waiting to hear." And he kissed her, a kiss that melted all her secret places, a kiss that made her whole body shimmer with heat.

When the kiss ended, she suggested softly, "We could go upstairs, or out to the workshop. …"

"You tempt me."

She chuckled. "Always."

He pressed his forehead to hers and he said in a husky whisper, "But I want to wait. Until you're my wife at last. I want you and Johnny and Sera to come live in my new place with me. Is that something you might consider? Letting me carry you across the threshold into the house on Catalpa Way?"

She lifted her mouth, brushed her lips across his. "I can't think of anything more right than that. Yes, let's go down to the courthouse as soon as it opens in the morning. And then let's get married right away. So we can make love in your bedroom in the house on Catalpa Way."

"*Our* bedroom," he corrected her.

"Yes, Bowie. Ours." She pulled him down to her, scooting over so he could sit beside her. He wrapped an arm around her. She snuggled in close.

They talked for a long time, about the life they would share, about the future that would be theirs. She told him all about Matteo and Emma and the carved box she'd found in the workshop.

Much later, when Sera woke, he went up and got her. And then after Sera had nursed, he took her upstairs again.

By then, Glory could barely keep her eyes open. She stretched out on the couch cushions and drifted off to sleep, waking only briefly when Bowie came down again and took her in his arms. She leaned her head on his shoulder, content in a way she'd never been in her life until that night.

Love will do that, she thought as sleep settled over her. It had taken a long time, some serious growing up on both their parts and a whole bunch of heartache. But in the end, love had made everything right.

The next morning, earlier than usual, Johnny came down the stairs and found his mother and father sound asleep on the sofa in the family room. Together.

He stood and stared at them.

When they just went on sleeping, he turned for the kitchen. He wasn't allowed to use the cooktop without an adult supervising. But he could fix his own cereal and get himself a glass of juice.

He ate his breakfast and he stared out the window by the table, thinking of the puppy he would be getting soon, of the bedroom in his dad's house where he could hear the river from his bed.

Johnny smiled. It was going to be a sunny day.

* * * * *

HEART & HOME

Heartwarming romances where love can
happen right when you least expect it.

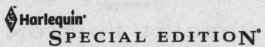

COMING NEXT MONTH
AVAILABLE FEBRUARY 28, 2012

#2173 MENDOZA'S MIRACLE
The Fortunes of Texas: Whirlwind Romance
Judy Duarte

#2174 A WEAVER PROPOSAL
Return to the Double C
Allison Leigh

#2175 THE LAST FIRST KISS
Matchmaking Mamas
Marie Ferrarella

#2176 DADDY ON HER DOORSTEP
McKinley Medics
Lilian Darcy

#2177 CLAIMING COLLEEN
Home to Harbor Town
Beth Kery

#2178 COURTING HIS FAVORITE NURSE
Lynne Marshall

You can find more information on upcoming Harlequin® titles,
free excerpts and more at www.HarlequinInsideRomance.com.

HSECNM0212

REQUEST YOUR FREE BOOKS!

2 FREE NOVELS PLUS 2 FREE GIFTS!

✦Harlequin·

SPECIAL EDITION

Life, Love & Family

YES! Please send me 2 FREE Harlequin® Special Edition novels and my 2 FREE gifts (gifts are worth about $10). After receiving them, if I don't wish to receive any more books, I can return the shipping statement marked "cancel." If I don't cancel, I will receive 6 brand-new novels every month and be billed just $4.49 per book in the U.S. or $5.24 per book in Canada. That's a saving of at least 14% off the cover price! It's quite a bargain! Shipping and handling is just 50¢ per book in the U.S. and 75¢ per book in Canada.* I understand that accepting the 2 free books and gifts places me under no obligation to buy anything. I can always return a shipment and cancel at any time. Even if I never buy another book, the two free books and gifts are mine to keep forever.

235/335 HDN FEGF

Name	(PLEASE PRINT)

Address	Apt. #

City	State/Prov.	Zip/Postal Code

Signature (if under 18, a parent or guardian must sign)

Mail to the Reader Service:
IN U.S.A.: P.O. Box 1867, Buffalo, NY 14240-1867
IN CANADA: P.O. Box 609, Fort Erie, Ontario L2A 5X3

Not valid for current subscribers to Harlequin Special Edition books.

Want to try two free books from another line?
Call 1-800-873-8635 or visit www.ReaderService.com.

* Terms and prices subject to change without notice. Prices do not include applicable taxes. Sales tax applicable in N.Y. Canadian residents will be charged applicable taxes. Offer not valid in Quebec. This offer is limited to one order per household. All orders subject to credit approval. Credit or debit balances in a customer's account(s) may be offset by any other outstanding balance owed by or to the customer. Please allow 4 to 6 weeks for delivery. Offer available while quantities last.

Your Privacy—The Reader Service is committed to protecting your privacy. Our Privacy Policy is available online at www.ReaderService.com or upon request from the Reader Service.

We make a portion of our mailing list available to reputable third parties that offer products we believe may interest you. If you prefer that we not exchange your name with third parties, or if you wish to clarify or modify your communication preferences, please visit us at www.ReaderService.com/consumerschoice or write to us at Reader Service Preference Service, P.O. Box 9062, Buffalo, NY 14269. Include your complete name and address.

HSE11B

Get swept away with author

CATHY GILLEN THACKER

and her new miniseries

Legends of Laramie County

On the Cartwright ranch, it's the women
who endure and run the ranch—and it's time for
lawyer Liz Cartwright to take over. Needing some help
around the ranch, Liz hires Travis Anderson, a fellow
attorney, and Liz's high-school boyfriend. Travis says
he wants to get back to his ranch roots, but Liz knows
Travis is running from something. Old feelings emerge
as they work together, but Liz can't help but wonder
if Travis is home to stay.

Reluctant Texas Rancher

**Available March
wherever books are sold.**

There came a time in a man's life when he knew he was well and truly caught. Devon Carter stared down at the diamond ring nestled in velvet and acknowledged that this was one such time. He snapped the lid closed and shoved the box into the breast pocket of his suit.

He had two choices. He could marry Ashley Copeland and fulfill his goal of merging his company with Copeland Hotels, thus creating the largest, most exclusive line of resorts in the world, or he could refuse and lose it all.

Put in that light, there wasn't much he could do except pop the question.

The doorman to his Manhattan high-rise apartment hurried to open the door as Devon strode toward the street. He took a deep breath before ducking into his car, and the driver pulled into traffic.

Tonight was the night. All of his careful wooing, the countless dinners, kisses that started brief and casual and became more breathless—all a lead-up to tonight. Tonight his seduction of Ashley Copeland would be complete, and then he'd ask her to marry him.

He shook his head as the absurdity of the situation hit him for the hundredth time. Personally, he thought William Copeland was crazy for forcing his daughter down Devon's throat.

Ashley was a sweet enough girl, but Devon had no desire

to marry anyone.

William had other plans. He'd told Devon that Ashley had no head for the family business. She was too softhearted, too naive. So he'd made Ashley part of the deal. The catch? Ashley wasn't to know of it. Which meant Devon was stuck playing stupid games.

Ashley was supposed to think this was a grand love match. She was a starry-eyed woman who preferred her animal-rescue foundation over board meetings, charts and financials for Copeland Hotels.

If she ever found out the truth, she wouldn't take it well.

And hell, he couldn't blame her.

But no matter the reason for his proposal, before the night was over, she'd have no doubts that she belonged to him.

What will happen when Devon marries Ashley?
Find out in Maya Banks's passionate new novel
TEMPTED BY HER INNOCENT KISS
Available March 2012 from Harlequin Desire!

HDEXP0312

Love Inspired

When Cat Barker ran away from the juvenile home she was raised in, she left more than an unstable childhood behind. She also left her first love, Jake Stone. Now, years later, Cat needs help, and there's only one person she can turn to—Jake, her daughter's secret father. Cat fears love and marriage but a daunting challenge renews her faith—and teaches them all a lesson about trust.

Lilac Wedding in Dry Creek
by Janet Tronstad

Available March wherever books are sold.

www.LoveInspiredBooks.com